SERENADE

James M. Cain

SERENADE

VINTAGE BOOKS

A DIVISION OF RANDOM HOUSE

NEW YORK

FIRST VINTAGE BOOKS EDITION, April 1978

Library of Congress Cataloging in Publication Data

Cain, James Mallahan, 1892-1977.
Serenade.

I. Title.
PZ3.C11993Se 1978 [PS3505.A3113] 813'.5'2
77-92634
ISBN 0-394-72585-9

Manufactured in the United States of America

Cover photo: Richard L. Shaefer

SERENADE

1

I WAS IN THE TUPINAMBA, having a *bizcocho* and coffee, when this girl came in. Everything about her said Indian, from the maroon *rebozo* to the black dress with purple flowers on it, to the swaying way she walked, that no woman ever got without carrying pots, bundles, and baskets on her head from the time she could crawl. But she wasn't any of the colors that Indians come in. She was almost white, with just the least dip of *café con leche*. Her shape was Indian, but not ugly. Most Indian women have a rope of muscle over their hips that give them a high-waisted, mis-shapen look, thin, bunchy legs, and too much breast-works. She had plenty in that line, but her hips were round, and her legs had a soft line to them. She was slim, but there was something voluptuous about her, like in three or four years she would get fat. All that, though, I only half saw. What I noticed was her face. It was flat, like an Indian's but the nose broke high, so it kind of went with the way she held her head, and the eyes weren't dumb, with that shiny, shoe-button look. They were pretty big, and black, but they leveled out straight, and had kind of a sleepy, impudent look to them. Her lips were thick, but pretty, and of course had plenty of lipstick on them.

It was about nine o'clock at night, and the place was pretty full, with bullfight managers, agents, newspaper men, pimps, cops and almost everybody you can think of, except somebody you would trust with your watch. She went to the bar and ordered a drink, then went to a table and sat down, and I had a stifled feeling I had had before, from the thin air up there, but that wasn't it this time. There hadn't been any woman in my life for quite some while, and I knew what this meant. Her drink came, and it was coca-cola and Scotch, and I thought that over. It might mean that she was just starting the evening, and it might mean she was just working up an appetite, and if it meant that I was sunk. The Tupinamba is more of a café than a restaurant, but plenty of people eat there, and if that was what she expected to do, my last three pesos wouldn't go very far.

I had about decided to take a chance and go over there when she moved. She slipped over to a place about two tables away, and then she moved again, and I saw what she was up to. She was closing in on a bullfighter named Triesca, a kid I had seen a couple of times in the ring, once when he was on the card with Solorzano, that seemed to be their main ace at the time, and once after the main season was over, when he killed two bulls in a novillada they had one Sunday in the rain. He was a wow with the cape, and just moving up into the money. He had on the striped suit a Mexican thinks is pretty nifty, and a cream-colored hat. He was alone, but the managers, agents, and writers kept dropping by his table. She didn't have much of a chance, but every time three or four or five of them would shove off she would slip nearer. Pretty soon she dropped down beside him. He didn't take off his hat. That ought to have told me something, but it didn't. All I saw was a cluck too stuck on himself to know how to act. She spoke, and he nodded, and they talked a little bit, and it didn't look like she had ever seen him before. She drank out, and he let it ride for a minute, then he ordered another.

When I got it, what she was in there for, I tried to lose interest in her, but my eyes kept coming back to her. After a few minutes, I knew she felt me there, and I knew some of the other tables had tumbled to what was going on. She kept pulling her *rebozo* around her, like it was cold, and hunching one shoulder up, so she half had

2

her back to me. All that did was throw her head up still higher, and I couldn't take my eyes off her at all. So of course a bullfighter is like any other ham, he's watching every table but his own, and he had no more sense than to see these looks that were going round. You understand, it's a dead-pan place, a big café with a lot of mugs sitting around with their hats on the back of their heads, eating, drinking, smoking, reading, and jabbering Spanish, and there wasn't any nudging, pointing, or hey-get-a-load-of-this. They strictly minded their business. Just the same, there would be a pair of eyes behind a newspaper that weren't on the newspaper, or maybe a waitress would stop by somebody, and say something, and there'd be a laugh just a little louder than a waitress's gag is generally worth. He sat there, with a kind of a foolish look on his face, snapping his fingernail against his glass, and then I felt a prickle go up my spine. He was getting up, he was coming over.

A guy with three pesos in his pocket doesn't want any trouble, and when the room froze like a stop-camera shot, I tried to tell myself to play it friendly, to get out of it without starting something I couldn't stop. But when he stood there in front of me he still had on that hat.

"My table, he interest you, ha?"

"Your—what?"

"My table. You look, you seem interest, Señor."

"Oh, now I understand."

I wasn't playing it friendly, I was playing it mean. I got up, with the best smile I could paste on my face, and waved at a chair. "Of course. I shall explain. I shall gladly explain." Down there you make it simple, because spig reception isn't any too good. "Please sit down."

He looked at me and he looked at the chair, but it looked like he had me on the run, so he sat down. I sat down. Then I did something I wanted to do for fifteen minutes. I lifted that cream hat off his head, like it was the nicest thing I knew to do for him, slipped a menu card under it, and put it on a chair. If he had moved I was going to let him have it, if they shot me for it. He didn't. It caught him by surprise. A buzz went over the room. The first round was mine.

3

"May I order you something, Señor?"

He blinked, and I don't think he even heard me. Then he began looking around for help. He was used to having a gallery yell Olé every time he wiped his nose, but it had walked out on him this time. It was all deadpan, what he saw, and so far as they were concerned, we weren't even there. There wasn't anything he could do but face me, and try to remember what he had come for.

"The explain. Begin, please."

I had caught him with one he wasn't looking for, and I decided to let him have another, right between the eyes. "Certainly. I did look, that is true. But not at you. Believe me, Señor, not at you. And not at the table. At the lady."

". . . You—tell me this? You tell me this thing?"

"Sure. Why not?"

Well, what was he going to do? He could challenge me to a duel, but they never heard of a duel in Mexico. He could take a poke at me, but I outweighed him by about fifty pounds. He could shoot me, but he didn't have any gun. I had broken all the rules. You're not supposed to talk like that in Mexico, and once you hand a Mexican something he never heard of, it takes him about a year to figure out the answer. He sat there blinking at me, and the red kept creeping over his ears and cheeks, and I gave him plenty of time to think of something, if he could, before I went on. "I tell you what, Señor. I have examined this lady with care, and I find her very lovely. I admire your taste. I envy your fortune. So let us put her in a lottery, and the lucky man wins. We'll each buy her a ticket, and the one holding the highest number buys her next drink. Yes?"

Another buzz went around, a long one this time. Not over half of them in there could speak any English, and it had to be translated around before they could get it. He took about four beats to think it through, and then he began to feel better. "Why I do this, please? The lady, she is with me, no? I put lady in lotería, what you put in, Señor? You tell me that?"

"I hope you're not afraid, Señor?"

He didn't like that so well. The red began to creep up

4

again, but then I felt something behind me, and I didn't like that so well either. In the U.S., you feel something behind you, it's probably a waiter with a plate of soup, but in Mexico it could be anything, and the last thing you want is exactly the best bet. About half the population of the country go around with pearl-handled automatics on their hips, and the bad part about those guns is that they shoot, and after they shoot nothing is ever done about it. This guy had a lot of friends. He was a popular idol, but I didn't know of anybody that would miss me. I sat looking straight at him, afraid even to turn around.

He felt it too, and a funny look came over his face. I leaned over to brush cigarette ashes off my coat, and out of the tail of my eye I peeped. There had been a couple of lottery peddlers in there, and when he came over they must have stopped in their tracks like everybody else. They were back there now, wig-wagging him to say yes, that it was in the bag. I didn't let on. I acted impatient, and sharpened up a bit when I jogged him. "Well, Señor? Yes?"

"Sí, sí. We make *lotería!*"

They broke pan then, and crowded around us, forty or fifty of them. So long as we meant business, it had to be hands off, but now that it was a kind of a game, anybody could get in it, and most of them did. But even before the crowd, the two lottery peddlers were in, one shoving pink tickets at me, the other green tickets at him. You understand; there's hundreds of lotteries in Mexico, some pink, some green, some yellow, and some blue, and not many of them pay anything. Both of them went through a hocus-pocus of holding napkins over the sheets of tickets, so we couldn't see the numbers, but my man kept whispering to me, and winking, meaning that his numbers were awful high. He was an Indian, with gray hair and a face like a chocolate saint, and you would have thought he couldn't possibly tell a lie. I thought of Cortés, and how easy he had seen through their tricks, and how lousy the tricks probably were.

But I was different from Cortés, because I wanted to be taken. Through the crowd I could see the girl, sitting there as though she had no idea what was going on, and

5

it was still her I was after, not getting the best of a dumb bullfighter. And something told me the last thing I ought to do was to win her in a lottery. So I made up my mind I was going to lose, and see what happened then.

I waved at him, meaning pick whatever one he wanted, and there wasn't much he could do but wave back. I picked the pink, and it was a peso, and I laid it down. When they tore off the ticket, they went through some more hocus-pocus of laying it down on the table, and covering it with my hat. He took the green, and it was half a peso. That was a big laugh, for some reason. They put his hat over it, and then we lifted the hats. I had No. 7. He had No. 100,000 and something. That was an Olé. I still don't get the chemistry of a Mexican. Out in the ring, when the bull comes in, they know that in exactly fifteen minutes that bull is going to be dead. Yet when the sword goes in, they yell like hell. And mind you, there's nothing as much like one dead bull as another dead bull. In that café that night there wasn't one man there that didn't know I was framed, and yet when the hats were lifted they gave him a hand, and clapped him on the shoulder, and laughed, just like Lady Luck had handed him a big victory.

"So. And now. You still look, ha?"

"Absolutely not. You've won, and I congratulate you, de todo corazón. Please give the lady her ticket, with my compliments, and tell her I hope she wins the Bank of Mexico."

"Sí, sí, sí. And so, Señor, adiós."

He went back with the tickets, and I put a little more hot leche into my coffee, and waited. I didn't look. But there was a mirror back of the bar, so I could see if I wanted to, and just once, after he had handed her the tickets, and they had a long jibber-jabber, she looked.

It was quite a while before they started out. I was between them and the door, but I never turned my head. Then I felt them stop, and she whispered to him, and he whispered back, and laughed. What the hell? He had licked me, hadn't he? He could afford to be generous. A whiff of her smell hit me in the face, and I knew she was

6

standing right beside me, but I didn't move till she spoke.

"Señor."

I got up and bowed. I was looking down at her, almost touching her. She was smaller than I had thought. The voluptuous lines, or maybe it was the way she held her head, fooled you.

"Señorita."

"*Gracias*, thanks, for the *billete*."

"It was nothing, Señorita. I hope it wins for you as much as it lost for me. You'll be rich—*muy rico*."

She liked that one. She laughed a little, and looked down, and looked up. "So. *Muchas gracias*."

"*De nada*."

But she laughed again before she turned away, and when I sat down my head was pounding, because that laugh, it sounded as though she had started to say something and then didn't, and I had this feeling there would be more. When I could trust myself to look around, he was still standing there near the door, looking a little sore. From the way he kept looking at the *damas*, I knew she must have gone in there, and he wasn't any too pleased about it.

In a minute, my waitress came and laid down my check. It was for sixty centavos. She had waited on me before, and she was a pretty little *mestiza*, about forty, with a wedding ring she kept flashing every time she got the chance. A wedding ring is big news in Mexico, but it still doesn't mean there's been a wedding. She pressed her belly against the table, and then I heard her voice, though her lips didn't move and she was looking off to one side: "The lady, you like her *dirección*, yes? Where she live?"

"You sure you know this *dirección*?"

"A *paraquito* have told me—just now."

"In that case, yes."

I laid a peso on the check. Her little black eyes crinkled up into a nice friendly smile, but she didn't move. I put the other peso on top of it. She took out her pencil, pulled the menu over, and started to write. She hadn't got three letters on paper before the pencil was jerked out of her hand, and he was standing there, purple with fury. He had tumbled, and all the things he had wanted to say to me, and never got the chance, he spit at her, and she spit back. I couldn't get all of it, but you couldn't miss the main points. He said she was delivering a message to me, she said she was only writing the address of a hotel I had asked for, a hotel for *Americanos*. They must like to see a guy framed in Mexico. About six of them chimed in and swore they had heard me ask her the address of a hotel, and that that was all she was giving me. They didn't fool him for a second. He was up his own alley now, and speaking his own language. He told them all where to get off, and in the middle of it, here she came, out of the *damas*. He let her have the last of it, and then he crumpled the menu card up and threw it in her face, and walked out. She hardly bothered to watch him go. She smiled at me, as though it was a pretty good joke, and I got up. "Señorita. Permit me to see you home."

That got a buzz, a laugh, and an Olé.

I don't think there's ever been a man so moony that a little bit of chill didn't come over him as soon as a woman said yes, and plenty of things were going through my head when she took my arm and we headed for the door of that café. One thing that was going through was that my last peso was gone at last, that I was flat broke in Mexico City with no idea what I was going to do or how I was going to do it. Another thing was that I didn't thank them for their Olé, that I hated Mexicans and their tricks, and hated them all the more because the tricks were all so bad you could always see through them. A Frenchman's tricks cost you three francs, but a Mexican is just dumb. But the main thing was a queer echo in that Olé, like they were laughing at me all the time, and I wondered, all of a sudden, which way we were going to turn when we got out that door. A girl on the make for a bullfighter, you don't exactly expect that she came out of a convent. Just the same, it hadn't occurred to me up to that second that she could be a downright piece of trade goods. I was hoping, when we reached the main street, that we would turn right. To the right lay the main part

8

of town, and if we headed that way, she could be taking me almost anywhere. But to our left lay the Guauhtemolzin, and that's nothing but trade.

We turned left.

We turned left, but she walked so nice and talked so sweet I started hoping again. Nothing about an Indian makes any sense. He can live in a hut made of sticks and mud, and sticks and mud are sticks and mud, aren't they? You can't make anything else out of them. But he'll take you in there with the nicest manners in the world, more dignity than you'd ever get from a dozen dentists in the U.S., with stucco bungalows that cost ten thousand dollars apiece, kids in a private school, and stock in the building and loan. She went along, her hand on my arm, and if she had been a duchess she couldn't have stepped cleaner. She made a little gag out of falling in step, looked up once or twice and smiled, and then asked me if I had been long in Mexico.

"Only three or four months."

"Oh. You like?"

"Very much." I didn't, but I wanted anyway to be as polite as she was. "It's very pretty."

"Yes." She had a funny way of saying yes, like the rest of them have. She drew it out, so it was "yayse." "Many flowers."

"And birds."

"And señoritas."

"I wouldn't know about them."

"No? Just a little bit?"

"No."

An American girl would have mauled it to death, but when she saw I didn't want to go on with it, she smiled and began talking about Xochimilco, where the best flowers grew. She asked me if I had been there. I said no, but maybe some day she would take me. She looked away at that, and I wondered why. I figured I had been a little previous. Tonight was tonight, and after that it would be time to talk about Xochimilco. We got to the Guauhtemolzin. I was hoping she would cross. She turned, and we hadn't gone twenty yards before she stopped at a crib.

I don't know if you know how it works in Mexico.

There's no houses, with a madame, a parlor, and an electric piano, anyway not in that part of town. There's a row of adobe huts, one story high, and washed blue, or pink, or green, or whatever it happens to be. Each hut is one room deep, and jammed up against each other in the way they are, they look like a barracks. In each hut is a door, with a half window in it, like a hat-check booth. Under the law they've got to keep that door shut, and drum up trade by leaning out the window, but if they know the cop they can get away with an open door. This door was wide open, with three girls in there, two of them around fourteen, and looking like children, the other big and fat, maybe twenty-five. She brought me right in, but then I was alone, because she and the other three went out in the street to have a palaver, and I could partly catch what it was. They all four rented the room together, so three of them had to wait outside when one of them had a customer, but I seemed to be a special case, and if I was going to spend the night, her friends had to flop somewhere else. Most of the street got in it before long, the cop, the café woman on the corner, and a flock of girls from the other cribs. Nobody sounded sore, or surprised, or made dirty cracks. A street like that is supposed to be tough, but from the way they talked, you would have thought it was the junior section of the Ladies' Aid figuring out where to bunk the minister's brother-in-law that had blown in town kind of sudden. They acted like it was the most natural thing in the world.

After a while they got it straightened out to suit them, who was to go where, and she came back and closed the door and closed the window. There was a bed in there, and a chest of drawers in the early Grand Rapids style, and a washstand with a mirror over it, and some grass mats rolled up in a corner, for sleeping purposes. Then there were a couple of chairs. I was tilted back on one, and as soon as she had given me a cigarette, she took the other. There we were. There was no use kidding myself any longer why Triesca hadn't taken off his hat. My lady love was a three-peso whore.

She lit my cigarette for me, and then her own, and inhaled, and let the smoke blow out the match. We smoked, and it was about as electric as a stalled car. Across the street in front of the café, a mariachi was playing, and she nodded her head once or twice, in time with the music. "Flowers, and birds—and mariachis."

"Yes, plenty of them."

"You like mariachi? We have them. We have them here."

"Señorita."

"Yes?"

". . . I haven't got the fifty centavos. To pay the mariachi. I'm—"

I pulled my pockets inside out, to show her. I thought I might as well get it over with. No use having her think she'd hooked a nice American sugar papa, and then letting her be disappointed. "Oh. How sweet."

"I'm trying to tell you I'm broke. Todo flat. I haven't got a centavo. I think I'd better be going."

"No money, but buy me billete."

"And that was the last of it."

"I have money. Little bit. Fifty centavos for mariachi. Now—you look so."

She turned around, lifted the black skirt, and fished in her stocking. Listen, I didn't want any mariachi outside the window, serenading us. Of all things I hated in Mexico, I think I hated the mariachis the worst, and they had come to make a kind of picture for me of the whole country and what was wrong with it. They're a bunch of bums, generally five of them, that would be a lot better off if they went to work, but instead of that they don't do a thing their whole life, from the time they're kids to the time they're old men, but go around plunking out music for anybody that'll pay them. The rate is fifty centavos a selection, which breaks down to ten centavos, or about three cents a man. Three play the violin, one the guitar, and one a kind of bass guitar they've got down there. As if that wasn't bad enough, they sing. Well, never mind how they sing. They gargle a bass falsetto that's enough to set your teeth on edge, but all music gets sung the way it deserves, and it was what they sang that got me down. You hear Mexico is musical. It's not. They do nothing

11

but screech from morning till night, but their music is the dullest, feeblest stuff that ever went down on paper, and not one decent bar was ever written there. Yeah, I know all about Chavez. Their music is Spanish music that went through the head of an Indian and came out again, and if you think it sounds the same after that, you made a mistake. An Indian, he's about eight thousand years behind the rest of us in the race towards whatever we're headed for, and it turns out that primitive man is not any fine, noble brute at all. He's just a poor fish. Modern man, in spite of all this talk about his being effete, can run faster, shoot straighter, eat more, live longer, and have a better time than all the primitive men that ever lived. And that difference, how it comes out in music. An Indian, even when he plays a regular tune, sounds like a seal playing My-Country-'Tis-of-Thee at a circus, but when he makes up a tune of his own, it just makes you sick.

Well, maybe you think I'm getting all steamed up over something that didn't amount to anything, but Mexico had done plenty to me, and all I'm trying to say is that if I had to listen to those five simple-looking mopes outside the window, there was going to be trouble. But I wanted to please her. I don't know if it was the way she took the news of my being broke, or the way her eyes lit up at the idea of hearing some music, or the flash I got of that pretty leg, when I was supposed to be looking the other way, or what. Whatever it was, her trade didn't seem to make much difference any more. I felt about her the way I had in the café, and wanted her to smile at me some more, and lean toward me when I spoke.

"Señorita."

"Yes?"

"I don't like the mariachi. They play very bad."

"Oh, yes. But they only poor boy. No estoddy, no take lessons. But play—very pretty."

"Well—never mind about that. You want some music that's the main thing. Let me be your mariachi."

"Oh—you sing?"

"Just a little bit."

"Yes, yes. I like—very much."

12

I went out, slipped across the street, and took the guitar from No. 4. He put up a squawk, but she was right after me, and he didn't squawk long. Then we went back. There's not many instruments I can't play, some kind of way, but I can really knock hell out of a guitar. He had it tuned cockeyed, but I brought it to E, A, D, G, B, and E without snapping any of his strings, and then I began to go to town on it. The first thing I played her was the prelude to the last act of Carmen. For my money, it's one of the greatest pieces of music ever written, and I had once made an arrangement of it. You may think that's impossible, but if you play that woodwind stuff up near the bridge, and the rest over the hole, the guitar will give you almost as much of what the music is trying to say as the whole orchestra will.

She was like a child while I was tuning, leaning over and watching everything I did, but when I started to play, she sat up and began to study me. She knew she had never heard anything like that, and I thought I saw the least bit of suspicion of me, as to who I was and what the hell I was doing there. So when I went down on the low E string, on the phrase the bassoon has in the orchestra, I looked at her and smiled. "The voice of the bull."

"Yes, yes!"

"Am I a good mariachi?"

"Oh, fine mariachi. What is the música?"

"Carmen."

"Oh. Oh yes, of course. The voice of the bull."

She laughed, and clapped her hands, and that seemed to do it. I went into the bullring music of the last act and kept stepping the key up, so I could make kind of a number out of it without slowing down for the vocal stuff. There came a knock on the door. She opened, and the mariachi was out there, and most of the ladies of the street. "They ask door open. So they hear too."

"All right, so they don't sing."

So we left the door open, and I got a hand after the bullring selection, and played the intermezzo, then the prelude to the opera. My fingers were a little sore, as I had no calluses, but I went into the introduction to the Habanera, and started to sing. I don't know how far I got.

13

What stopped me was the look on her face. Everything I had seen there was gone, it was the face at the window of every whorehouse in the world, and it was looking right through me.

" . . . What's the matter?"

I tried to make it sound comical, but she didn't laugh. She kept looking at me, and she came over, took the guitar from me, went out and handed it to the *mariachi* player. The crowd began to jabber and drift off. She came back, and the other three girls were with her. "Well, Señorita—you don't seem to like my singing."

"Muchas gracias, Señor. Thanks."

"Well—I'm sorry. Good evening, Señorita."

"Buenos noches, Señor."

Next thing I knew I was stumbling down the Bolivar, trying to wash her out of my mind, trying to wash everything out of my mind. A block away, somebody was coming toward me. I saw it was Triesca. She must have gone out and phoned him when I left. I ducked around a corner, so I wouldn't have to pass him. I kept on, crossed a plaza, and found myself looking at the Palacio de Bellas Artes, their opera house. I hadn't been near it since I flopped there three months before. I stood staring at it, and thought how far I had slid. Flopping in Rigoletto, in probably the lousiest opera company in the world, before an audience that didn't know Rigoletto from Yankee Doodle, with a chorus of Indians behind me trying to look like lords and ladies, a Mexican tenor on one side of me that couldn't even get a hand on *Questa o Quella*, and a coffee cake on the other side that scratched fleas while she was singing the *Caro Nome*—that seemed about as low as I could get. But I had wiped those footprints out, with my can. I had tried to serenade a lady that was easy serenaded, and I couldn't even get away with that.

I walked back to my one-peso hotel, where I was paid up to the end of the week, went to my room, and undressed without turning on the light, so I wouldn't see the concrete floor, the wash basin with rings in it, and the lizard that would come out from behind the bureau. I

14

got in bed, pulled the lousy cotton blanket up over me, and lay there watching the fog creep in. When I closed my eyes I'd see her looking at me, seeing something in me, I didn't know what, and then I'd open them again and look at the fog. After a while it came to me that I was afraid of what she saw in me. There would be something horrible mixed up in it, and I didn't want to know what it was.

2

As WELL AS I CAN REMEMBER, that was in June, and I didn't see her for a couple of months. Never mind what I did in that time, to eat. Sometimes I didn't eat. For a while I had a job in a jazzband, playing a guitar. It was in a nightclub out on the Reforma, and they needed me bad. I mean, the place was for Americans, and the music they handed out was supposed to be the McCoy, but it wasn't. I went to work, and got them so they could play the hot stuff hot and the blue stuff blue, anyway a little bit, and polished up a couple of them so they could take a solo strain now and then, just for variety. Understand, you couldn't do much. A Mexican's got a defective sense of rhythm. He sounds rhythmic on the *cucaracha* stuff, but when you slow him down to foxtrot time, he can't feel it. He just plays it mechanically, so when people get out on the floor they can't dance to it. Still, I did what I could, and figured a few combos that made them sound better than they really were, and business picked up. But then a guy with a pistol on his hip showed up one night and wanted to see my papers, and I got thrown out. They got Socialism down there now, and one of the rules is that Mexico belongs to the Mexicans. They're out of luck, no matter how they play it. Under Diaz, they turned the country over to the foreigners, and they had prosperity, but the local boys didn't get much of it. Then they had the Revolution, and fixed it up so that whatever was going on, the local boys had to run it. The only trouble is, the local boys don't seem to be very good at it. They threw me out, and then they had Socialism, but they didn't have any jazzband. Business fell off, and later I heard the place closed.

After that, I even had to beg to stay on at the hotel until I got the money from New York, which wasn't ever coming, as they knew as well as I did. They let me use the room, but wouldn't give me any bedclothes or service. I had to sleep on the mattress, under my clothes, and haul my own water. Up to then, I had managed to keep some kind of press in my pants, so I could anyway bum a meal off some American in Butch's café, but I couldn't even do that any more, and I began to look like what I was, a beachcomber in a spig town. I wouldn't even have eaten if it hadn't been for shagging my own water. I started going after it in the morning, and because the tin pitcher wouldn't fit under the tap in the washroom at the end of the hall, I had to go down to the kitchen. Nobody paid any attention to me, and then an idea hit me, and next time I went down at night. There was nobody there, and I ducked over to the icebox. They've got electric iceboxes all over Mexico, and some of them have combinations on them, like safes, but this one hadn't. I opened it up, and a light went on, and sure enough, there was a lot of cold stuff in there. I scooped some frijoles into a glass ashtray I had brought down, and held them under the pitcher when I went up. When I got back to my room I dug into them with my knife. After that, for two weeks, that was what I lived on. I found ten centavos in the street one day, and bought a tin spoon, a clay soapdish, and a cake of soap. The soapdish and the soap I put on the washstand, like they were some improvements of my own I was putting in, since they wouldn't give me any. The spoon I kept in my pocket. Every night when I'd go down, I'd scoop beans, rice, or whatever they had, and sometimes a little meat into the soapdish, but only when there was enough that it wouldn't be missed. I never touched anything that might have counted, and only took off the top of dishes where there was quite a lot of it, and then smoothed them up to look right. Once there was half a Mexican ham in there. I cut myself off a little piece, under the butt.

And then one morning I got this letter, all neatly typewritten, even down to the signature, on a sheet of white business paper.

Calle Guauhtemolzin 44b,
Mexico, D. F.
A 14 de agosto.

Sr. John Howard Sharp,
Hotel Dominguez,
Calle Violeta,
Ciudad.
Mi Querido Jonny:

En vista de que no fue posible verte ayer en el mercado al ir a las compras que ordinariamente hago para la casa en donde trabajo, me veo precidada para dirigirte la presente y manifestarte que dormí inquieta con motivo de tus palabras me son vida y no pudiendo permanecer sin contacto contigo te digo que hoy por la noche te espero a las ocho de la noche para que platiquemos, por lo que así espero estaras presente y formal.

Se despide quien te ama de todo corazón y no te olivida,

JUANA MONTES

How she got my name and address didn't bother me. The waitress at the Tupinamba would have been good for that. But the rest of it, the date I was supposed to have with her yesterday, and how she couldn't sleep for thinking about me, didn't make any sense at all. Still, she wanted to see me, that seemed to be the main point, and it was a long time before sundown. I was down past the point where I cared how she had looked at me, or what it meant, or anything like that. She could look at me like I was a rattlesnake, for all I cared, so she had a couple of buns under the bed. I went back upstairs, shaved, and started up there, hoping something about it might lead to a meal.

When I rapped on the door the window opened, and

the fat one poked her head out. The four of them were just getting up. The window closed, and Juana called something out to me. I waited, and pretty soon she came out. She had on a white dress this time, that must have cost all of two pesos, and white socklets, and shoes. She looked like some high school girl in a border town. I said hello and how had she been, she said very well, gracias, and how had I been? I said I couldn't complain, and edged toward the door to see if I could smell coffee. There didn't seem to be any. Then I took out the letter and asked her what it meant.

"Yes. I ask you to come. Yes."

"I caught that. But what's all this other stuff about? I didn't have any date with you—that I know of."

She kept studying me, and studying the letter, and hungry as I was, and bad as she had walloped me that night, and dumb as it had been up to now, I couldn't help having this same feeling about her I had had before, that was mainly what any man feels toward a woman, but partly what he feels toward a child. There was something about the way she talked, the way she held her head, the way she did everything, that got me in the throat, so I couldn't breathe right. It wasn't child, of course. It was Indian. But it did things to me just the same, maybe worse on account of it being Indian, because that meant she was always going to be like that. The trouble was, you see, that she didn't know what the letter said. She couldn't read.

She called the fat one out, and had her read it, and then there was the most indignant jabbering you ever heard. The other two came out and got in it, and then she grabbed me by the arm. "The auto. You make go, yes?"

"Well, I could once."

"Come, then. Come quick."

We went down the street, and she turned in at a shack that seemed to be a kind of a garage. It was full of wrecks with stickers pasted on the windshield, that seemed to be held for the sheriff or something, but halfway down the line was the newest, reddest Ford in the world. It shone like a boil on a sailor's neck. She went up to it, and began

18

waving the letter in one hand and the key in the other. "So. Now we go. Calle Venezuela."

I got in, and she got in, and it was a little stiff, but it started, and I rolled it through the murk to the street. I didn't know where the Calle Venezuela was, and she tried to show me, but she didn't have the hang of the one-way streets, so we got tangled up so bad it took us a half hour to get there. As soon as I backed up to park she jumped out and ran over to a colonnade, where about fifty guys were camped out on the sidewalk, back of tables with typewriters on them. They all wore black suits. In Mexico, the black suit means you got plenty of education, and the black fingernails mean you got plenty of work. When I got there, she was having an argument with one guy, and after a while he sat down to his machine, stuck a piece of paper in it, wrote something, and handed it to her. She came over to me waving it, and I took it. It was just two lines, that started off "Querido Sr. Sharp" instead of "Querido Jonny," and said she wanted to see me on a matter of business.

"This letter, big mistake."

She tore it up.

Well, never mind the fine points. The result of the big Socialist educational program is that half the population of the city have to come to these mugs to get their letters written, and that was what she had done. But the guy had been a little busy, and didn't get it quite straight what she had said, and fixed her up with a love letter. So of course, she had to go down there and get what she had paid for. I didn't blame her, but I still didn't know what she wanted, and I was still hungry.

"The auto—you like, yes?"

"It's a knockout." We were coming up the Bolivar again, and I had to keep tooting the horn, according to law. The main thing they put on cars for Mexican export is the biggest, loudest horn they can find in Detroit, and this one had a double note to it that sounded like a couple of ferryboats passing in an East River fog. "Your business must be good."

19

I didn't mean to make any crack, but it slipped out on me. If it meant anything to her at all, she passed it up.

"Oh no. I win."

"How?"

"The *billete*. You remember?"

"Oh. My *billete*?"

"Yes. I win, in *lotería*. The auto, and five honnerd pesos. The auto, is very pretty. I can no make go."

"Well, I can make it go, if that's all that's bothering you. About those five hundred pesos. You got some of them with you?"

"Oh yes. Of course."

"That's great. What you're going to do is buy me a breakfast. For my belly—*muy* empty. You get it?"

"Oh, why you no say? Yes, of course, now we eat."

I pulled in at the Tupinamba. The restaurants don't open until one o'clock, but the cafés will take care of you. We took a table up near the corner, where it was dark and cool. Hardly anybody was in there. My same old waitress came around grinning, and I didn't waste any time. "Orange juice, the biggest you got. Fried eggs, three of them, and fried ham. Tortillas. Glass of milk, *frío*, and *café con crema*."

"*Bueno*."

She took iced coffee, a nifty down there, and gave me a cigarette. It was the first I had had in three days, and I inhaled and leaned back, and smiled at her. "So."

"So."

But she didn't smile back, and looked away as soon as she said it. It was the first time we had really looked at each other all morning, and it brought us back to that night. She smoked, and looked up once or twice to say something, and didn't, and I saw there was something on her mind besides the *billete*. "So—you still have no pesos?"

"That's more or less correct."

"You work, no?"

"I did work, but I got kicked out. Just at present, I'm not doing anything at all."

"You like to work, yes? For me?"

". . . Doing what?"

"Play a guitar, little bit, maybe. Write a letter, count money, speak *Inglés*, help me, no work very hard. In Mexico, nobody work very hard. Yes? You like?"

"Wait a minute. I don't get this."

"Now I have money, I open house."

"Here?"

"No, no, no. In Acapulco. In Acapulco, I have very nice friend, big *político*. Open nice house, with nice music, nice food, nice drink, nice girls—for American."

"Oh, for Americans."

"Yes. Many Americans come now to Acapulco. Big steam-boat stop there. Nice man, much money."

"And me, I'm to be a kind of a combination professor, bartender, bouncer, glad-hander, secretary, and general bookkeeper for the joint, it that it?"

"Yes, yes."

"Well."

The food came along, and I stayed with it a while, but the more I thought about her proposition the funnier it got to me. "This place, it's supposed to have class, is that the idea?"

"Oh yes, very much. My *político* friend, he say American pay as much as five pesos, gladly."

"Pay five—what?"

"Pesos."

"Listen, tell your *político* friend to shut his trap and let an expert talk. If an American paid less than five dollars, he'd think there was something wrong with it."

"I think you little bit crazy."

"I said five bucks—eighteen pesos."

"No, no. You kid me."

"All right, go broke your own way. Hire your *político* for manager."

"You really mean?"

"I raise my right hand and swear by the holy mother of God. But—you got to get some system in it. You got to give him something for his money."

"Yes, yes. Of course."

"Listen, I'm not talking about this world's goods. I'm talking about things of the spirit, romance, adventure, beauty. Say, I'm beginning to see possibilities in this. All

21

right, you want that American dough, and I'll tell you what you've got to do to get it. In the first place, the dump has got to be in a nice location, in among the hotels, not back of the coconut palms, up on the hill. That's up to your *político*. In the second place, you don't do anything but run a little dance hall, and rent rooms. The girls came in, just for a drink. Not mescal, not tequila. Chocolate ice-cream soda, because they're nice girls. that just dropped in to take a load off their feet. They wear hats. They come in two at a time, because they're so well brought up they wouldn't dream of going in any place alone. They work in the steamboat office, up the street, or maybe they go to school and just came home for vacation. And they've never met any Americans, see, and they're gigling about it, in their simple girlish way, and of course, we fix it up, you and I, so there's a little introducing around. And they dance. And one thing leads to another. And next thing you know, the American has a room from you, to take the girl up. You don't really run that kind of place, but just because it's him, you'll make an exception—for five dollars. The girl doesn't take anything. She does it for love, see?"

"For *what*?"

"Do I know the Americano, or don't I?"

"I think you just talk, so sound fonny."

"It sounds fonny, but it's not just talk. The Americano, he doesn't mind paying for a room, but when it comes to a girl, he likes to feel it's a tribute to his personality. He likes to think it's a big night for her, too, and all the more because she's just a poor little thing in a steamboat office, and never had such a night in her life until he came along and showed her what life could be like with a real guy. He wants an adventure—with him the hero. He wants to have something to tell his friends. But don't have any bums sliding up to take their *foto*. He doesn't like that."

"Why not? The *fotógrafo*, he pay me little bit."

"Well, I tell you. Maybe the *fotógrafo* has a heart of gold, and so has the *muchacha*, but the Americano figures the *foto* might get back to his wife, or threaten to, specially if she's staying up at the hotel. He wants an adventure, but he doesn't want any headache. Besides, the *fotos* have got a Coney Island look to them, and might give him the idea it was a cheap joint. Remember, this place has class. And that reminds me, the *mariachi* is going to be hand-picked by me, and hand-trained as well, so maybe somebody could dance to the stuff when they play it. Of course, I don't render any selections on the guitar. That's out. Or the piano, or the violin, or any other instrument in my practically unlimited repertoire. And that *mariachi*, they wear suits that we give them, with gold braid down the pants, and turn those suits in every night when they quit. It's our own private *mariachi*, and as fast as we get money to buy more suits we put on more men, so it's a feature. The main thing is that we have class, first, last, and all the time. No Americano, from the time he goes in to the time he goes out, is going to get the idea that he can get out of spending money. Once they get that through their heads, we'll be all right."

"The Americanos, are they all crazy?"

"All crazy as loons."

It seemed to be settled, but after the gags wore off I had this sick feeling, like life had turned the gray-white color of their sunlight. I tried to tell myself it was the air, that'll do it to you at least three times a day. Then I tried to tell myself it was what I had done, that I had no more pride left than to take a job as pimp in a coast-town whorehouse, but what the hell? That was just making myself look noble. It was, anyway, some kind of work, and if I really made a go of it, it wouldn't make me squirm. It would make me laugh. And then I knew it was this thing that was drilling in the back of my head, about her. There hadn't been a word about that night, and when she looked at me her eyes were just as blank as though I'd been some guy she was talking to about the rent. But I knew what those eyes could say. Whatever it was she had seen in me that night, she still saw it, and it was between us like some glass door that we could see through but couldn't talk.

She was sitting there, looking at her coffee glass and

23

not saying anything. She had a way of dozing off like that, between the talk, like some kitten that falls asleep as soon as you stop playing with it. I told you she looked like some high school girl in that little white dress. I kept looking at her, trying to figure out how old she was, when all of a sudden I forgot about that and my heart began to pound. If she was to be the madame of the joint, she couldn't very well take care of any customers herself, could she? Then who was going to take care of her? By her looks, she needed plenty of care. Maybe that was supposed to be my job. My voice didn't quite sound like it generally does when I spoke to her.

". . . Señorita, what do I get out of this?"

"Oh—you live, have nice cloth, maybe big hat with silver, yes? Some pesos. Is enough, yes?"

"—And entertain the señoritas?"

I don't know why I said that. It was the second mean slice I had taken since we started out. Maybe I was hoping she'd flash jealous, and that would give me the cue I wanted. She didn't. She smiled, and studied me for a minute, and I felt myself getting cold when I saw there was the least bit of pity in it. "If you like to entertain señoritas, yes. Maybe not. Maybe that's why I ask you. No have any trouble."

3

EARLY NEXT MORNING I shaved, washed, and packed. My earthly possessions seemed to be a razor, brush, and cake of soap, two extra shirts, a pair of extra drawers I had washed out the night before, a pile of old magazines, and the black-snake whip I had used when I sang Alfio. They give you a whip, but it never cracks, and I got this mule-skinner's number with about two pounds of lead in the butt. One night on the double bill a stagehand laid it out for Pagliacci, and the Nedda hit me in the face with it. I still carry the scar. I had sold off all the costumes and scores, but couldn't get rid of the whip. I dropped it in the suitcase. The magazines and my new soap-dish I put on top of it, and stood the suitcase in the corner. Some day, maybe, I would come back for it. The two extra shirts I put on, and tied the necktie over the top one. The extra drawers I folded and put in one pocket, the shaving stuff in another. I didn't mention I was leaving, to the clerk, on my way out. I just waved at him, like I was on my way up to the postoffice to see if the money had come, but I had to slap my hand against my leg, quick. She had dropped a handful of pesos in my pocket, and I was afraid he'd hear them clink.

The Ford was an open roadster, and I lost a half hour getting the boot off and the top up. It was an all-day run to Acapulco, and I didn't mean to have that sun beating down on me. Then I rolled it out and pulled down to 44b. She was on the doorstep, waiting for me, her stuff piled up around her. The other girls weren't up yet. She was all dressed up in the black dress with purple flowers that she had had on when I first saw her, though I thought the white would have been better. The main baggage seemed to be a round hatbox, of the kind women traveled with fifteen years ago, only made of straw and stuffed full of clothes. I peeled off the extra shirts and put them and the hatbox in the rumble seat. Then there was the grass mat that she slept on, rolled up and tied. I stuck that in, but it meant I couldn't close the rumble. Those mats, they sell for sixty centavos, or maybe twenty cents, and it didn't hardly look like it was worth the space, but it was a personal matter, and I didn't want to argue. Then there was a pile of rebozos, about every color there was, but mainly black. I put them in, but she ran out and took one, a dark purple, and threw it over her head. Then there was the cape, the espada, and the ear. It was the first time I ever saw a bullfighter's cape, the dress cape, I mean, not the fighting cape, up close so I could really look at it. I hated it because I knew where she had got it, but you couldn't laugh off the beauty of

25

it. I think it's the only decently made thing you'll ever see in Mexico, and maybe it's not even made there. It's heavy silk, each side a different color, and embroidered so thick it feels crusty in your hands. This one was yellow outside, crimson in, and against that yellow the needlework just glittered. It was all flowers and leaves, but not in the dumb patterns you see on most of their stuff. They were oil-painting flowers, not postcard flowers, and the colors had a real tone to them. I folded it, put a *rebozo* around it, to protect it from dust, and laid it beside the hatbox. The *espada*, to me, was just one more grand-opera prop. It's what they use to stick the bull with, and I didn't even take it out of the scabbard to look at it. I threw it down in the bottom.

While I was loading the stuff in, she was standing there stroking the ear. I wouldn't have handled it with tongs. Sometimes, when a bullfighter puts on a good show, they give him an ear. The crowd begins to yell about it, and then one of the assistants goes over and cuts an ear off the bull, where he's lying in the dirt with the mules hooking on to his horns. The bullfighter takes it, holds it up so you can see all the blood and slime, and goes around with it, bowing every ten steps. Then he saves it, like a coloratura saves her decoration from the King of Belgium. After about three months it's good and rank. This one she had, there were pieces of gristle hanging out of it, and it stunk so you could smell it five feet away. I told her if it went on the front seat with us the deal was off, and she could throw it back there with the *espada*. She did, but she was plenty puzzled.

The window popped open then, and the fat one showed, with some kind of a nightgown on, and her hair all frazzled and ropy, and then the others ones were beside her, and there was a lot of whispering and kissing, and then we got in and got started. We lost about ten minutes, out on the edge of town, when we stopped to gas up, and another five when we came to a church and she had to go in and bless herself, but finally, around eight o'clock we leveled off. We passed some wooden crosses, another little feature they've got. Under Socialism, it seems that there's only one guy that really knows how it works, and if some other guy thinks he does, it's a counter-revolutionary act, or, in unsocialist lingo, treason. So back in 1927, a guy named Serrano thought he did, and they arrested him and his friends down in Cuernavaca, and started up to Mexico with them in a truck. But then up in Mexico somebody decided it would be a good idea if they never got there at all, and some of the boys started out in a fast car to meet them. They fastened their hands with baling wire, lined them up beside the road, and mowed them down with a machine gun. Then they said the revolution was over, and the American papers handed it to them that they had a stable government at last, and that a strong man could turn the trick, just give him the chance. So wooden crosses mark the spot, an inspiring sight to see.

We had some coffee in Cuernavaca, then pushed on to Taxco for lunch. That was the end of the good road. From there on it was just dust, curves, and hills. She began to get sleepy. A Mexican is going to sleep at one o'clock, no matter where he is, and she was no exception. She leaned her head against the side, and her eyes drooped. She wriggled, trying to get set. She slipped off her shoes. She wiggled some more. She took off a string of beads around her neck, and unfastened two buttons. She was open to her brassiere. Her dress slipped up, above her knees. I tried not to look. It was getting hotter by the minute. I didn't look, but I could smell her.

I gassed in Chilpancingo, around four o'clock, and bathed the tires with water. That was what I was afraid of, mostly, that in that heat and sliding all over that rough road, we would have a blow-out. I peeled down to my undershirt, knotted a handkerchief around my head to catch sweat, and we went on. She was awake now. She didn't have much to say. She slipped off her stockings, held her bare legs in the air stream from the hood vent, and unbuttoned another button.

We were down in what they call the *tierra caliente*, now, and it turned cloudy and so muggy the sweat stood out on my arms in drops. After Chilpancingo I had been looking for some relief, but this was the worst yet. We had been running maybe an hour when she began to lean forward and look out, and then she told me to stop. "Yes. This way."

I rubbed the sweat out of my eyes and looked, and saw something that maybe was intended to be a road. It was three inches deep in dust, and cactuses were growing in the middle of it, but if you concentrated we could see two tracks. "That way, hell. Acapulco is the way we're going. I looked it up."

"We go for Mamma."

". . . What was that you said?"

"Yes. Mama will cook. She cook for us. For the house in Acapulco."

"Oh, I see."

"Mamma cook very nice."

"Listen. I haven't had the honor of meeting Mamma, but I've just got a hunch she's not the type. Not for the high-class joint we're going to run. I tell you what. Let's get down there. If worse comes to worst, I'll cook. I cook very nice, too. I studied in Paris, where all the good cooks go when they die."

"But Mamma, she have the *viveres*."

"The what?"

"The food, what we need. I send Mamma the money, I sent last week. She buy much things, we take. We take Mamma, Papa. All the *viveres*."

"Oh, Papa too."

"Yes, Papa help Mamma cook."

"Well, will you tell me where you, me, Mamma, Papa, and the *viveres* are going to ride? By the way, do we take the goat?"

"Yes, this way, please."

It was her car, and I turned into the road. I had gone about a hundred yards when the wheel jerked out of my hands and I had to stamp on the brake to keep from going down a gully that must have been two hundred feet deep. I mean, it was that rough, and it didn't get any better. It was uphill and down, around rocks the size of a truck, through gullies that would have bent the axles of anything but a Ford, over cactuses so high I was afraid they would foul the transmission when we went over

28

them. I don't know how far we went. We drove about an hour, and the rate we were moving, it might have been five miles or twenty, but it seemed more like fifty. We passed a church and then a long while after that, we began to pass Mexicans with burros, hurrying along with them. That's a little point about driving in Mexico they don't tell you about. You meet these herds of burros, going along loaded up with wood, fodder, Mexicans, or whatever it is. The burro alone doesn't give you much trouble. He knows the rules of the road as well as you do, and gets out of the way in time, even if he's a little grouchy about it. But if he's got a Mexican herding him along, you can bet on it that that Mexican will shove him right in line with your fender and you do nothing but stand on your brake and curse and sweat and cake up with their dust.

It was the way they were hurrying along, though, that woke me up to what it looked like outside. The heat and dust were enough to strangle you, but the clouds were hanging lower all the time, and over the tops of the ridges smoky scuds were slipping past, and it didn't look good. After a long time we passed some huts, by twos and threes, huddled together. We kept on, and then we came to a couple more huts, but only one of them seemed to have anybody in it. She reached over and banged on the horn and jumped out, and ran up to the door, and all of a sudden there was Mamma, and right behind her, Papa. Mamma was about the color of a copper pot, all dressed up in a pink cotton dress and no shoes, to go to Acapulco. Papa was a little darker. He was a nice, rice mahogany after it's had about fifteen coats of dark polish. He came out in his white pajama suit, with the pants rolled up to his bare knees, and took off his big straw hat and shook hands. I shook hands. I wondered if there had been a white iceman in the family. Then I pulled up the brake and got out.

Well, I said she ran up to the door, but that wasn't quite right. There wasn't any door. Maybe you never saw an Indian hut, so I better tell you what it looks like. You can start with the colored shanties down near the railroad track in New Orleans, and then, when you've got them clearly in mind, you can imagine they're the Waldorf-Astoria Hotel, and that the Mexican hut is a shanty standing beside it. There's no walls, or roofs, or anything like you're used to seeing. There's four sides made of sticks, stuck down in the ground and wattled together with twigs, about as high as a man's head. In the middle of the front side is a break, and that's the door. The chinks between the twigs are filled up a little bit with mud. Just plain mud, smeared on there and most of it falling off. And on top is a thatch of grass, or palmetto, or whatever grows up on the hill, and that's all. There's no windows, no floor, no furniture, no pictures of the Grand Canyon hanging on the walls, no hay-grain-and-feed calendars back of the clock, with a portrait of a cowgirl on top of a horse. They've got no need for calendars, because in the first place they couldn't figure out what the writing was for, and in the second place they don't care what day it is. And they've got no need for a clock, because they don't care what time it is. All I'm trying to say is, there's nothing in there but a dirt floor, and the mats they sleep on, and down near the door, the fire where they do their cooking.

So that was where she came from, and she ran in there, barefooted like they were, and began to laugh and talk, and pat a dog that showed up in a minute, and act like any other girl that's come home after a trip to the city. It went on quite a while, but the clouds weren't hanging any higher, and I began to get nervous. "Listen, this is all very well, but how about the *viveres*?"

"Yes, yes. Mamma have buy very good estoff."

"Fine, but let's get it aboard."

It seemed to be stored in the other hut, the one that nobody was living in. Papa ducked in there and began to carry out iron plates for cooking tortillas, machetes, pots, and jars and such stuff. One or two of them were copper, but most of them were pottery, and Mexican pottery means the worst pottery in the world. Then Mamma showed up with baskets of black beans, rice, ground corn, and eggs. I stowed the stuff in the rumble seat, shoving the pots in first. But pretty soon it was chock up to the top, and, when I came to the baskets I had to lash them to the side with some twine that they had so they rode the running board. Some of the stuff, like the charcoal, wasn't even in baskets. It was done up in bundles. I lashed that too. The eggs I finally found a place for in back, on top of her hatbox. Each egg was wrapped in cornhusk, and I figured they would ride all right there and not break.

Then Papa came grinning out with a bundle, bigger than he was, of brand-new mats, all rolled up and tied. I couldn't figure out why they were so nuts about mats, but later I found out. He mussed up my whole rumble seat by dragging out the mat she had brought, unrolling his pile, rolling out her mat with the others and tying them up again. Then he lashed them to the side on top of the charcoal. I stood on the fender, grabbed the top and rocked the car. The twine broke and the mats fell out in the dirt. He laughed over that. They got a funny sense of humor. Then he got a wise look on his face, like he knew how to fix it, and went out back of the hut. When he showed again he was leading a burro, all saddled up with a rack. He opened the mats again, split them into two piles and rolled them separate. Then he lashed them to the burro, one pile on each side. Then he led the burro to the car and tied him to the rear bumper.

I untied the burro, took the mats off him, and rolled them into one pile again. I lifted them. They weren't so heavy. I hoisted them on to the top so one end was on the top, the other on the rumble seat, where it was open, and lashed them on to the top brace. I went in the hut. Juan was tying up one more basket, the old lady squatting on the stove bricks, smoking a cigar. She jumped up, ran out the door and around back, and came back with a bone. Juana had to untie the basket again, and in it was the dog. The old lady dropped the bone in, Juana put the top on and tied it up.

I went out, took the key out of my pocket, got in, and started the car. I had to back up to turn around, and all three of them started to scream and yell. It wasn't Spanish. I think it was pure Aztec. But you could get the drift. I was stealing the car, the *viveres*, everything they had.

Up to then I was nothing but a guy going nuts, and trying to get started in time to get there if we ever were going to get there. But the way they acted gave me an idea. I put her in first, hauled out of there, and kept on going.

Juana was right after me, screaming at the top of her voice, and jumped on the running board. "You estop! You steal auto! You steal *viveres*. You estop! You estop now!"

I did like hell stop. I stayed in first, so she wouldn't get shaken off, but I kept on over the hill, sounding like a load of tin cans with all that stuff back there, until Mamma and Papa were *todo* out of sight. Then I threw out and pulled up the brake.

"Listen, Juana. I'm not stealing your car. I'm not stealing anything—though why the hell you couldn't have bought all this stuff in Acapulco where you could get it cheap, instead of loading up here with it, that's something I don't quite understand. But get this: Mamma, and Papa and the burro, and that dog—they're not coming."

"Mamma, she cook, she—"

"Not tonight she doesn't. Tomorrow maybe we'll come back and get her, though I doubt it. Tonight I'm off, right now. I'm on my way. Now if you want to come—"

"So, you steal my car, yes."

"Let's say borrow it. Now make up your mind."

I opened the door. She got in. I switched on the lights and we started.

By that time I would say it was about seven o'clock. It was dark from the clouds, but it still wasn't night. There was a place down the line called Tierra Colorada that we might make before the storm broke, if I could ever get back to the main road. I had never been there, but it looked like there would be some kind of a hotel, or anyway cover for the car, with all that stuff in it. I began to force. I had to go up the hills in first, but coming down I'd let her go, with just the motor holding her. It was rough, but the clock said 20, which was pretty good. Well, you take a chance on a road like that, you're headed for a fall. All of a sudden there was a crash and a jerk, and we stopped. I pedaled the throttle. The motor was dead. I pulled the starter, and she went. We had just hit a rock, and stalled. But after that I had to go slower.

Up to then I was still sweating from the air and the work. So was she. Then we topped a rise and it was like we had driven into an icebox. She shivered and buttoned her dress. I had just about decided I would have to stop and put on my coat when we drove into it. No sheet of water, nothing like that. It just started to rain, but it was driving in on her side, and I pulled up. I put on my coat, then made her get out and lifted up the seat to get the side curtains. I felt around in there with my hand. There wasn't a wrench, a jack, or tool of any kind, and not a piece of a side curtain.

"Nice garage you picked."

In Mexico you even have to have a lock on your gasoline tank. It was a wonder they hadn't even stripped her of the lights.

We got in and started off. By now it was raining hard, and most of it coming in on her. While I was hunting for curtains she had dug out a couple of *rebozos* and wrapped them around her, but even that woven stuff stuck to her like she had just come out of a swimming pool. "Here. You better take my coat."

"No, *gracias*."

It seemed funny, in the middle of all that, to hear that soft voice, those Indian manners.

The dust had turned to grease, and off to the right, down near the sea, you could hear the rumble of thunder, how far off you couldn't tell, with the car making all that noise. I wrestled her along. Every tilt down was a skid, every tilt up was a battle, and every level piece was a wrench, where you were lifting her out of holes she went in, up to her axles. We were sliding around a knob with the hill hanging over us on one side, and dropping under us on the other, so deep you couldn't see the bottom. The drop was on my side, and I had my eyes glued to the road, crawling three feet at a time, because if we took a skid there it was the end. There was a chock overhead, all the top braces strained, and something went bouncing down the gully the size of a five-gallon jug. I was on the brake before it hit the ground, and after a long time I heard her breathe. The engine was still running and I went on. It must have been a minute before I figured out what that was. The rain had loosened a rock above us, and it came down. But instead of coming through and killing us, it had hit the end of the mat roll and glanced off.

It cut the fabric, though, and as soon as we rounded the knob that was the end of the top. The wind got under it, and it ripped and the rain poured down on me. It was coming from my side now. Then the mats began to roll, and there came another rip, and it poured down on her.

"Very bad."

"Not so good."

We passed the church, and started down the hill. I had to use brake and motor to hold her, but down at the bottom it looked a little better ahead, so I lifted my foot to give her the gun. Then I stamped on the brake so hard we stalled cold. What lay ahead, in the rain, looked like a wet sand flat where I could make pretty good time. What it was was yellow water, boiling down the arroyo so fast that it hardly made a ripple. Two more feet and we would have been in, up to the radiator. I got out, went around the car and found I had a few feet clear behind. I got in, started, and backed. When I could turn around I did, and went sliding up the hill again, the way we had come. Where we were going I didn't know. We couldn't get to Tierra Colorado, or Acapulco, or any place we wanted to go, that was a cinch. We were cut off. And whether we could make Mamma's hut, or any hut, was plenty doubtful. With the top flapping in ribbons, and all that water beating in, that motor was due to short any minute, and where that would leave us I hated to think.

We got to the top of the hill and started down the other side, past the church. Then I woke up. "All right, get in the church there, out of the wet. I'll be right after you."

"Yes, yes."

She jumped out and ran down there. I pulled off to one side, set the brake, and fished out my knife. I was going to cut those mats loose and use some of them to blanket the motor, and some of them to protect the seat and stuff in back until I could carry it in there. But the main thing I thought about was the car. If that didn't go, we were sunk. While I was still trying to get the knife open with my wet fingernail she was back. "Is close."

"What was that?"

"The church, is close. Is lock. Now we go on, yes. We go back to Mamma."

"We will like hell."

I ran over to the doors, shook them and kicked them. They were big double doors and they were locked all right. I tried to think of some way I could get them open. If I had a jack handle I could have shoved it in the crack and pried, but there wasn't any jack handle. I beat on the doors and cursed them, and then I went back to the car. The engine was still running and she was sitting in it. I jumped in, turned, and pointed it straight at the church. The steps didn't bother me. The church was below the road and they went down, instead of up, and anyway they were just low tile risers, about three inches high, and pretty wide. When she saw what I was going to do, she began to whimper, and beg me not to, and grabbed the wheel to make me stop. "No, no! Not the *Casa de Dios*, please, no! We go back! We go back to Mamma."

I pushed her away and eased the front wheels down the first step. I bumped them down the next two steps, and then the back wheels came down with a slam. But I was still rolling. I kept on until the front bumper was against the doors. I stayed in first, spun the motor, and little by little let in the clutch. For three or four seconds nothing happened, but I knew something had to crack. It did. There came a snap, and I was on the brake. If those doors opened outward I didn't want to tear out their hinges.

I backed up the width of the last step, pegged her there with the brake and got out. The bolt socket had torn out. I pulled the doors open, shoved Juana in, went back and started to work on the mats again. Then I thought, what's the matter with you? Don't be a fool. I ran back and pulled the doors as wide open as they would go. Then I ran in and began to drag pews around, working by the car lights, until there was an open space right up the center aisle. Then I went back and drove the car right in there. I went back and pulled the doors shut. The headlights were blazing right at the Blessed Sacrament, and she was on her knees at the altar rail, begging forgiveness for the sacrilegio.

I sat down in one of the pews where it was turned sidewise, just to sit. I began to worry about the car lights. At the time it seemed I was thinking about the battery, but it may have been the Blessed Sacrament, boring into the side of my head, I don't know. I got up and cut them. Right away the roar of the rain was five times as loud. In with it you could hear the rumble of thunder, but you couldn't see any lightning. It was pitch dark in there, except for one red spot. The sacristy light was burning. From up near it came a moan. I had to have light. I cut the switch on again.

Off to one side of the altar was what looked like a vestry room. I went back there. The water squirted out of my shoes when I walked. I took them off. Then I took off my pants. I looked around. There was a cassock hanging there, and some surplices. I took off everything, wet undershirt, wet drawers, wet socks, and put on the cassock. Then I took a lighter that was standing in a corner and started out to the sacristy lamp. I knew my matches wouldn't work. Walking on a tile floor barefoot you don't make much noise, and when she saw me with the lighter, in the cassock, I don't know what she thought, or if she thought. She fell on her face in front of me and began to gibber, calling me padre and begging for absolutión. "I'm not the padre, Juana. Look at me. It's me."

"Ah, Díos!"

"I'm lighting the candles so we can see."

But I mumbled it low. I pulled down the lamp, lit the

lighter and slipped it up again. Then I went around through the vestry room and up on the altar and lit three candles on one side, crossed over and lit three on the other. I cut the lighter, went back to the vestry room, put it in its place again. Then I went back and cut the car lights.

One funny thing about that that I didn't realize until I snapped that switch. Each time I crossed that altar I went down on one knee. I stood there, looking at the six candles I had lit, and thought that over. It had been twenty years, ever since I had been a boy soprano around Chicago, since I had thought of myself as a Catholic. But they knock it into you. Some of it's there to stay.

I lifted eggs and about fifteen other things from the rumble, until I could get out her hatbox. It was pretty wet but not as wet as the rest of the stuff. I took it back to the vestry room, set it down, then went out and touched her on the shoulder. "Your things are back there. You better get out of that wet dress."

She didn't move.

By that time it must have been about half past eight, and it dawned on me that why I felt so lousy was that I was hungry. I got a candle off the altar, lit it, went back and stuck it to the rear fender of the car, and took stock. I lifted out most of that stuff from the rumble seat, and unlashed what was riding the running board, and all I could see that was doing us any good was the eggs. I unwrapped one and took out my knife to puncture the end so I could suck it, and then I noticed the charcoal. That gave me an idea. There were some loose tiles in the floor and I clawed up a couple of them and carried them to the vestry room and stood them on their sides. Then I got one of the iron plates for cooking tortillas, and laid it across them and carried in the charcoal.

Next thing was how I was going to cook the eggs. There were no skillets or anything like that. And I went through every basket there was and there wasn't any butter, grease or anything you could use for grease. But there was a copper pot, bigger than I wanted but anyway a pot, so that meant that anyway I could boil the eggs. While I was rooting through those beans and rice and stuff that would take all night to cook, I smelled coffee and started looking for it. Finally I hit it, buried in with the rice in a paper bag, and then I found a little coffee pot. The coffee wasn't ground, but there was a metate there for grinding corn, and I mashed up a couple of handfuls with that, and put it in a bowl.

I went in the vestry room with what I had and the next thing was what I was going to use for water. It was dripping through every seam in the room and running down the windows in streams, but it looked kind of tough to get enough of it to cook. Still, I had to get some. Out back I could hear a stream pouring off the roof, so I took the biggest of the bowls and pulled the bolt on the rear door, right back of the altar. But when I opened it I could see a well, just a few steps down the hill. I took off the cassock. It was the only dry thing there was, and I wasn't letting it get wet. I went down to the well stark naked. The rain came down on me like a needle shower and at first it was terrible, but then it felt good. I threw out my chest against it and let it beat me. Then I pulled up the bucket and poured the water in the bowl. When I got back in the church with it I was running water even from my eyeballs. I felt around back of the altar for a closet. Oh, it was coming back to me, fast. I knew where they kept everything. Sure enough, I found a door and opened it, and there they were, the altar cloths, all in a neat pile. I took one, rubbed myself dry with it and put on the cassock. It was warm. I began to feel better.

The choir loft was off to one side and I started there to get a hymn book, so I could tear it up to start the fire. Then I changed my mind. Except for the window, there was no vent in the vestry room, and I didn't want to be smoked out, right at the start. I took four or five pieces of charcoal, laid them in a little pile between my tiles, went back to the altar and got another candle. I held the flame under the charcoal, turning all the time to keep the melting even, and pretty soon I got a little glow. I fed a couple more pieces on, and it glowed still redder. In a minute it was off, and I blew out the candle. There was hardly any smoke. Charcoal doesn't make much.

I laid the plate over the tiles, put the pot on it, and dipped some water in the pot. Then I dropped in some eggs. I started with six, but then I kept thinking how hungry I was, and I wound up with a dozen. I filled the coffee pot, scooped in some coffee, and put that on. Then I sat there, feeding the fire and waiting for the eggs to boil. They never did. The pot was too big or the fire too small, or something. The most I got was smoke coming off the top, but they were cooking all the time, so I didn't worry much. Anyway, they'd be hot. But the coffee boiled. The old smell hit me in the nose, and when I lifted the lid the grounds were simmering around. I took an egg, went to the back door, broke it, and let the egg spill out on the ground. The shell I took back and dropped in the coffee. That was what it needed. It began to clear.

I watched the eggs some more, and then I thought about my cigarettes and matches. They were in my coat, and I went to the car to get it. Then I thought about her things. I put the cigarettes and matches on the end of the tortilla plate to dry. Her stuff I took out of the hatbox and draped them near the fire on a bench that was back there. What she had I could only half see. It was all damp, but it smelled like her. One dress was wool, and I put that nearest the heat, and a pair of shoes, on the floor near it. Then I got to wondering how we were going to eat the eggs, even if they ever got cooked. There were no spoons or anything like that, and I always hated eggs out of the shell. I went out to the car again and half filled a little bowl with corn meal. I came back, dipped a little water into it. I worked it with my fingers, and when it got pasty I patted some of it into a tortilla, or anyway into some kind of a flapjack that was big enough to hold an egg. I put it on the plate to cook, and when it began to turn color I turned it over. When it was done on both sides I tasted it. It didn't taste right. I went out and got some salt I had found and forgotten to take. I mixed a little salt in, tried another one, and anyway you could eat it. Pretty soon I had twelve. That was one for each egg, and I thought that was enough.

All that took a long time, and there wasn't one peep out of her the whole time I was at work. She had moved from the altar rail to a pew, but she was still out there, a *rebozo* over her head and her bare feet sticking out behind, where she was kneeling with her face in her hands. I slid in the pew, took her by the arm and led her into the vestry room. "I told you once to take off that wet dress. Here's one that's fairly dry, and you go back there and change it. If your underwear's wet, you better take it off."

I picked up the woolen dress and shoved her behind the altar with it. When she came back she had it on. "Sit on the bench so your feet will be on the warm tiles near the fire. When those shoes are dry you can put them on."

She didn't. She sat on the bench, but with her back to the fire, so her feet were on cold tiles. That was so she could face the altar. She dropped her head in her hands and began to mutter. I got out my knife, broke an egg tortilla, and shoved it at her. The egg was half hard and half soft, but it rode the tortilla all right.

She shook her head. I put the tortilla down, went to the altar, got three or four candles, lit them, came back and stuck them around. Then I closed the door, the one that led to the altar and that I had kept open, to have more light. That kind of blocked her off on the muttering and she half turned around. When she saw the tortillas she laughed. That seemed to help. "Look very fonny."

"Well, maybe they look fonny but I didn't notice you doing much about them. Anyway, you can eat them."

She picked up the tortilla, half wrapped it around the egg and bit into it. "Taste very fonny."

"The hell it does."

I had bit into my first one by then, and it hit the spot. We wolfed them down. She ate five and I ate seven. We were talking in a natural tone of voice for the first time since we got in out of the storm, and it came to me it was because that door that led to the altar was shut. I got up and closed the other door, the one leading into the church, and that made it still better. We got to the coffee and there was nothing we could drink it out of but one little bowl, so we took turns. She would take a guzzle and then I would. In a minute I reached for the cigarettes. They were dry, and so were the matches. We lit up and inhaled. They tasted good.

"You feel better now?"

"Yes, gracias. Was very cold, very hongry."

"You still worried about the sacrilegio?"

"No, not now."

"There wasn't any sacrilegio, you know."

"Yes, very bad."

"No, not a bit. It's the Casa de Díos, you know. Everybody's welcome in here. You've seen the burros in here, haven't you? And the goats? On the way to market? The car is just the same. If we had to break the door in, that was only because we didn't have any key. I showed plenty of respect, didn't I? You saw me genuflect every time I crossed, didn't you?"

"Genu—"

"Bow—in front of the Host?"

"Yes, of course."

"No sacrilegio there, was there? You're all upset about nothing. Don't worry, I know. I know as much about it as you do. More probably."

"Very bad sacrilegio. But I pray. Soon, I confess. I confess to the padre. Then, absolución. No bad any more."

By that time it must have been somewhere around eleven o'clock at night. The rain hadn't let up, but sometimes it would be heavy, sometimes not so bad. The thunder and lightning would come up and go. There must have been three or four storms rolling up those canyons from the sea, and we'd get it, and it would die away and then we'd get it again. One was coming up now. She began to do what I'd noticed her doing once in the car, hold her breath and then speak, after a second or two when you could almost hear her heart beat. I tumbled that the sacrilegio was only part of what was eating on her. Most of it was the storm. "The lightning bother you?"

"No. The trueno, very bad."

It didn't look like it would pay to try to explain to her that the lightning was the works, the thunder nothing but noise, so I didn't try. "Try to sing a little. That generally helps. You know *La Sandunga?*"

"Yes, very pretty."

"You sing and I'll be *mariachi.*"

I began to drum on the bench and do a double shuffle with my feet. She opened her mouth to sing, but there came a big clap of thunder just then, and she didn't quite make it. "Outside, I no feel afraid. I like. Is very pretty."

"A lot of people are like that."

"Home, with Mamma, I no feel afraid."

"Well—that's practically outside, at that."

"Here, afraid, very much. I think about the *sacrilegio,* think about many things. I feel very bad."

You couldn't blame her much because it wasn't exactly what you'd call a gay place. I understood how she felt. I felt a little that way myself.

"Anyhow, it's dry. In spots."

The lightning came and I put my arm around her. The thunder broke and the candles guttered. She put her head on my shoulder and hid her face in my neck.

It died off after a while and she sat up. I opened the window a crack to get a little oxygen in the air, and put a couple more sticks of charcoal on the fire. "You had a good dinner?"

"Yes, gracias."

"You feel like a little work?"

". . . Work?"

"Suppose you be fixing us up a place to sleep while I wash up."

"Oh yes—gladly."

I went and brought the mats and and then got out a pile of altar cloths. Then I took the pots, bowls, and water out back and washed them up. I couldn't see very well, but I did the best I could. I had to duck out to the well once or twice, stripped down like I was before, and rub off with the same old cloth, so it took me about a half hour. When I got done I piled the things up inside the door and went in there. She was already in bed. She had taken

42

three or four of the mats and some altar cloths, for herself, and bedded me down across the room.

I blew out the candles we had eaten by, and stepped out on the altar to blow out the ones I had lit there, and then I noticed the other one, the one I had stuck to the car fender, was still burning. I stepped over the rail, went back there and blew it out. Then I started up to the altar again. My legs felt queer and shaky. I slipped in a pew and sat down.

I knew what it was all right, and it came to me then why I had put her to fixing the mats and taken all that time to wash up. I had hoped she would just fix one bed, and then when she didn't, it was like a wallop in the pit of the stomach to me. I had even quit wondering why I was the only man on the face of the earth she wouldn't sleep with. What I hated was that it made any difference to me.

I don't know how long I sat there. I wanted to smoke, and I had the cigarettes and matches with me, but I just held them in my hand. I was over by the choir loft, out of line with the Blessed Sacrament, but I was right in line with the crucifix, and I couldn't make myself light up. Another storm began to come up. I enjoyed it that she was across there in the vestry room, all alone, and scared to death. It kept rolling up, the worst we had had yet. There came two flashes of lightning, and then one terrific shot of thunder right after them. The candles were just guttering up again when there came a blaze of lightning, and the thunder right with it, and every candle up there went out. For a second you couldn't see a thing but the red spot of the sacristy lamp.

Then she began to scream. From where she was, with the door to the altar open like I had left it, maybe she caught it sooner than I did. Or maybe for a split second I had my eyes closed. I don't know. Anyway, the church filled with green light, and then it seemed to settle over the crucifix, so the face looked alive, like it was going to cry out. Then you couldn't see anything but the red spot.

She was screaming her head off now, and I had to have light. I dived for the choir loft, scratched a match, and lit

43

the organ candles. I don't know how many there were. I lit them all, so it was a blaze of candles. Then I turned to go and light the altar candles again, but I would have to cross in front of the crucifix and I couldn't do it. All of a sudden I sat down to the organ. It was a small pedal organ, and I pumped with my bare feet and started to play. I kept jerking out stops, to make it louder. The thunder rolled, and the louder it rolled the louder I played. I didn't know what I was playing, but after a while I knew it was an *Agnus Dei*. I cut it off and started a *Gloria*. It was louder. The thunder died off and the rain came down like all Niagara was over us. I played the *Gloria* over again.

"Sing."

I couldn't see her. She was outside the circle of light, where I was sitting in the middle. But I could feel her, up at the altar rail again, and if singing was what she wanted, that suited me too. I skipped the *Qui Tollis* the *Quoniam*, and the rest of it down to the *Credo*, and went on from there. Don't ask me what it was. Some of it was Mozart, some of it was Bach, some of it was anybody you can think of. I must have sung a hundred masses in my time, and I didn't care which one it was, so I could go on without a break. I went straight through to the *Dona Nobis*, and played off soft after I finished it, and then I stopped. The lightning and thunder had stopped again, and the rain was back to its regular drumming.

"Yes."

She just whispered it, but she drew it out like she always did, so the end of it was a long hiss. ". . . Just like the priest."

My head began to pound like it would split. That was the crown of skunk cabbage, all right, after all the years at harmony, of sight-reading, of piano, of light opera, of grand opera in Italy, Germany and France—to be told by this Indian that couldn't even read that I sounded like a priest. And it didn't help any that that was just what I sounded like. The echo of my voice was still in my ears and there was no getting around it. It had the same wooden, dull quality that a priest's voice has, without one

44

particle of life in it, one echo that would make you like it.

My head kept pounding. I tried to think of something to say that would rip back at her, and couldn't.

I got up, blew out all the candles but one, and took that one with me. I started up past the crucifix to cross over to the vestry room. She wasn't at the crucifix. She was out in front of the altar. At the foot of the crucifix I saw something funny and held the candle to see what it was. It was three eggs, in a bowl. Beside them was a bowl of coffee and a bowl of ground corn. They hadn't been there before. Did you ever hear of a Catholic putting eggs, coffee, and corn at the foot of the cross? No, and you never will. That's how an Aztec treats a god.

I crossed over, and stood behind her, where she was crouched down, on her knees, her face touching the floor and her hands pressing down beside it. She was stark naked, except for a *rebozo* over her head and shoulders. There she was at last, stripped to what God put there. She had been sliding back to the jungle ever since she took off that first shoe, coming out of Taxco, and now she was right in it.

A white spot from the sacristy lamp kept moving back and forth, on her hip. A creepy feeling began to go up my back, and then my head began to pound again, like sledge hammers were inside of it. I blew out the candle, knelt down, and turned her over.

4

WHEN IT WAS OVER we lay there, panting. Whatever it was that she had done to me, that the rest of it had done to me, I was even. She got up and went back to the car. There was some rattling back there, and then I felt her

45

coming back, and got up to meet her. I was getting used to the dark by then, and I saw the flash of a machete. She came in on a run, and when she was a couple of yards away she took a two-handed chop with it. I stepped back and it pulled her off balance. I stepped in, pinned her arms, and pressed my thumb against the back of her hand, right at the wrist. The knife fell on the floor. She tried to wriggle free. Mind you, neither one of us had a stitch on. I tightened with one arm, lifted her, carried her in the vestry room and closed both doors. Then I dumped her in the bed she had been in, piled in with her, and pulled up the covers. The fire still made a little glow, and I lit a cigarette and I smoked it, holding her with the other arm, then squashed it against the floor.

When she tired, I loosened up a little, to let her blow. Yes, it was rape, but only technical, brother, only technical. Above the waist, maybe she was worried about the sacrilegio, but from the waist down she wanted me, bad. There couldn't be any doubt about that.

There couldn't be any doubt about it, and it kind of put an end to the talk. We lay there, then, and I had another cigarette. I squashed it out, and from away off there came a rumble of thunder, just one. She wriggled into my arms, and next thing I knew it was daylight, and she was still there. She opened her eyes, closed them again, and came closer. Of course there wasn't but one thing to do about that, so I did it. Next time I woke up I knew it must be late, because I was hungry as hell.

It rained all that day, and the next. We split up on the cooking after the first breakfast. I did the eggs and she did the tortillas, and that seemed to work better. I got the pot to boil at last by setting it right on the tiles without any plate, and it not only made it boil, but saved time. In between, though, there wasn't much to do, so we did whatever appealed to us.

The afternoon of the second day it let up for about a half hour, and we slid down in the mud to have a look at the arroyo. It was a torrent. No chance of making Acapulco that night. We went up the hill and the sun came out plenty hot. When we got to the church the rocks back of it were alive with lizards. There was every size lizard you could think of, from little ones that were transparent like shrimps, to big ones three feet long. They were a kind of a blue gray, and moved so fast you could hardly follow them with your eyes. They leveled out with their tail, somehow, so they went over the rocks in a straight line, and almost seemed to fly. Looking at them you could believe it all right, that they turned into birds just by letting their scales grow into feathers. You could almost believe it that they were half bird already.

We climbed down and stood looking at them, when all of a sudden she began to scream. "Iguana! Iguana! Look, look, big iguana!"

I looked, and couldn't see anything. Then, still as the rock it was lying on, and just about the color of it, I saw the evilest-looking thing I ever laid eyes on. It looked like some prehistoric monster you see in the encyclopedia, between two and three feet long, with a scruff of spines that started at its head and went clear down its back, and a look in its eye like something in a nightmare. She had grabbed up a little tree that had washed out by the roots, and was closing in on him. "What are you doing? Let that goddam thing alone!"

When I spoke he shot out for the next rock like something on springs, but she made a swipe and caught him in mid-air. He landed about ten feet away, with his yellow belly showing and all four legs churning him around in circles. She scrambled over, hit him again, and then she grabbed him. "Machete! Quick, bring machete!"

"Machete, hell, let him go I tell you!"

"Is iguana! We cook! We eat!"

"Eat!—that thing?"

"The machete, the machete!"

He was scratching her by that time, and if she wouldn't let him go I wasn't letting him make hash out of her. I dove in the church for the machete. But then some memory of this animal caught me. I don't know whether it was something I had read in Cortés, or Diaz, or Martyr, or somebody, about how they cooked it when the Aztecs still ran Mexico, or some instinct I had

47

brought away from Paris, or what. All I knew was that if we ever cut his head off he was going to be dead, and maybe that wouldn't be right. I didn't grab a machete. I grabbed a basket, with a top on it, and dug out there with it. "The machete! The machete, give me machete!"

He had come to by now, and was fighting all he knew, but I grabbed him. The only place to grab him was in the belly, on account of those spines on his back, and that put his claws right up your arm. She was bleeding up to her elbows, and now it was my turn. Never mind how he felt and how he stunk. It was enough to turn your stomach. But I gave him the squeeze, shoved him head-down in the basket, and clapped the top on. Then I held it tight with both hands.

"Get some twine."

"But the machete! Why no bring—"

"Never mind. I'm doing this. Twine—string—that the things were tied with."

I carried him in, and she got some twine, and I tied the top on, tight. Then I set him down and tried to think. She didn't make any sense out of it, but she let me alone. In a minute I fed up the fire, took the pot out and filled it with water. It had started to rain again. I came in and put the pot on to heat. It took a long while. Inside the basket those claws were ripping at the wicker, and I wondered if it would hold.

At last I got a simmer, and then I took the pot off and got another basket-top ready. I picked him up, held him way above my head, and dropped him to the floor. I remembered what shock did to him the first time, and I hoped it would work again. It didn't. When I cut the string and grabbed, I got teeth, but I held on and socked him in the pot. I whipped the basket-top on and held it with my knee. For three seconds it was like I had dropped an electric fan in there, but then it stopped. I took the top off and fished him out. He was dead, or as dead as a reptile ever gets. Then I found out why it was that something had told me to put him in the pot alive, and not cook him dead, with his head cut off, like she wanted to do. When he hit that scalding water he let go.

He purged, and that meant he was clean inside as a whistle.

I went out, emptied the pot, heated a little more water, and scrubbed it clean with cornhusks, from the eggs. Then I scrubbed him off. Then I filled the pot, or about two thirds filled it, with clean water, and put it on the fire. When it began to smoke I dropped him in. "But is very fonny. Mamma no cook that way."

"Is fonny, but inspiration has hit me. Never mind how Mamma does it. This is how I do it, and I think it's going to be good."

I fed up the fire, and pretty soon it boiled. I cut it down to a simmer, and this smell began to come off it. It was a stink, and yet it smelled right, like I knew it was going to smell. I let it cook along, and every now and then I'd fish him up and pull one of his claws. When a claw pulled out I figured he was done. I took him out and put him in a bowl. She reached for the pot to go out and empty it. I almost fainted. "Let that water alone. Leave it there, right where it is."

I cut off his head, opened his belly, and cleaned him. I saved his liver, and was plenty careful how I dissected off the gall bladder. Then I skinned him and took off the meat. The best of it was along the back and down the tail, but I carved the legs too, so as not to miss anything. The meat and liver I stowed in a little bowl. The guts I threw out. The bones I put back in the pot and fed up the fire again, so it began to simmer. "You better make yourself comfortable. It's a long time before dinner."

I aimed to boil about half that water away. It began to get dark and we lit the candles and watched and smelled. I washed off three eggs and dropped them in. When they were hard I fished them out, peeled them, and laid them in a bowl with the meat. She pounded up some coffee. After a long time that soup was almost done. Then something popped into my mind. "Listen, we got any paprika?"

"No, no paprika."

"Gee, we ought to have paprika."

"Pepper, salt, yes. No paprika."

"Go out there to the car and have a look. This stuff needs paprika, and it would be a shame not to have it just because we didn't look."

"I go, but is no paprika."

She took a candle and went back to the car. I didn't need any paprika. But I wanted to get rid of her so I could pull off something without any more talk about the sacrilegio. I took a candle and a machete and went back of the altar. There were four or five closets back there, and a couple of them were locked. I slipped the machete blade into one and snapped the lock. It was full of firecrackers for high mass and stuff for the Christmas chèche. I broke into another one. There it was, what I was looking for, six or eight bottles of sacramental wine. I grabbed a bottle, closed the closets, and came back. I dug the cork out with my knife and tasted it. It was A-1 sherry. I socked about a pint in the pot and hid the bottle. As soon as it heated up a little I lifted the pot off, dropped the meat in, sliced up the eggs, and put them in. I sprinkled in some salt and a little pepper.

She came back. "Is no paprika."

"It's all right. We don't need it. Dinner's ready."

We dug in.

Well, brother, you can have your Terrapin Maryland. It's a noble dish, but it's not Iguana John Howard Sharp. The meat is a little like chicken, a little like frog-legs, and a little like muskrat, but it's tenderer than any of them. The soup is one of the great soups of the world, and I've eaten Marseilles bouillabaisse, New Orleans crayfish bisque, clear green turtle, thick green turtle, and all kinds of other turtle there are. I think it was still better that we had to drink it out of bowls, and fish the meat out with a knife. It's gelatinous, and flooding up over your lips, it makes them sticky, so you can feel it as well as taste it. She drank hers stretched out on her belly, and after a while it occurred to me that if I got down and stuck my mouth up against hers, we would be stuck, so we experiemented on that for a while. Then we drank some more soup, ate some more meat, and made the coffee. While we were drinking that she started to laugh. "Yeh? And what's so funny?"

"I feel—how you say? Dronk?"

"Probably born that way."

"I think you find wine. I think you steal wine, put in iguana."

"Well?"

"I like, very much."

"Why didn't you say so sooner?"

So I got out the bottle, and we began to swig it out of the neck. Pretty soon we were smearing her nipples with soup, to see if they would stick. Then after a while we just lay there, and laughed.

"You like the dinner?"

"It was lovely dinner, gracias."

"You like the cook?"

"Yes. . . . Yes. . . . Yes. Very fonny cook."

God knows what time it was when we got up from there and went out front to wash up. She helped me this time, and when we opened the door it had stopped raining and the moon was shining. That set us off again. After we got the stuff clean we started to laugh and dance out there in the mud, barefooted. I started to hum some music for it, and then I stopped. She was standing out there in the glare of the moon with that same look on her face she had the first night I met her. But she didn't turn away from me this time. She came closer and looked at me hard. "Sing."

"Oh, the hell with it."

"No, please, sing."

I started over again, what I had been humming, but this time I sang it, instead of humming it, and then I stopped again. It didn't sound like a priest any more. I walked over to the edge of the rocks and threw one down the arroyo, with a wide-open throttle. I don't know what it was. It came full and round, the way it once had, and felt free and good. I cut, and had just taken breath for another one when the echo of the first one came back to me. I caught my breath. That echo had something in it my voice had never had before, some touch of sweetness, or excitement, or whatever it was, that I had always

51

lacked. I cut the second one loose, and she came over and stood looking at me. I kept throwing them, each one tone higher than the last. I must have got up to F above the staff. Then I did a turn in the middle of my voice and shot one as high as I dared. When the echo came it had a ring to it almost like a tenor. I turned and ran into the church and up to the organ, to check pitch. It was A flat, and church organs are always high. At orchestra pitch, it was at least an A natural.

I was trembling so bad my fingers shook on the keys. Listen, I was never a great baritone. I guess you begin to place me by now, and after the Don Giovanni revival, and especially after the Hudson-to-Horn hookup, you heard I was the greatest since Bispham, and some more stuff like that. That was all hooey. I was no Battistini, no Amato, no John Charles Thomas. On voice, I was somewhere between Bonelli and Tibbett. On acting, I was pretty good. On music, I was still better. On singing, I was as good as they come. I ought to be, seeing it was all I ever did, my whole life. But never mind all that. I had a hell of a good voice, that's all I'm trying to say, and I had worked on it, lived for it, and let it be a part of me until it was a lot more than just something to make a living with. And I want you to get it straight why it was when this thing happened in Europe, and it cracked up on me for no reason that I could see, and then when I got sold down to Mexico as a broken-down hack that couldn't be sent any place better, and then when I wasn't even good enough for that,—it wasn't only that I was a bum, and down and out. Something in me had died. And now that it had come back, just as sudden as it went, I was a lot more excited than you would be if you found a hundred-dollar bill somewhere. I was more like a man that had gone blind, and then woke up one morning to find out that he could see.

I played an introduction, and started to sing. It was *Eri Tu*, from Ballo in Maschera. But I couldn't be bothered with pedaling that old wreck. I walked out in the aisle, and walked around with it, singing without accompaniment. I finished it, sang it again, and checked pitch. It had pulled a little sharp. That was right, after that long lay-off, it ought to do that. I played a chord for pitch, and started another. I sang for an hour, and hated to quit, but at that high pitch an hour was the limit.

She sat in a pew, staring at me as I walked around. The sacreligio didn't seem to bother her much any more. When I stopped, she came in the vestry room with me, and we dropped off what we had on, and lay down. There were six or seven cigarettes left. I kept smoking them. She lay beside me, up on one elbow, still staring at me. When the cigarettes were gone I closed my eyes and tried to go to sleep. She opened one eye, with her finger, and then the the other eye. "That was very beautiful, gracias."

"I used to be a singer."

"Yes. Maybe I made a mistake."

"I think you did."

". . . Maybe not."

She kissed me then, and went to sleep. But the fire was dead, the moon had gone down, and the window was gray before I went to sleep.

5

WE PULLED INTO ACAPULCO the next afternoon around five thirty. We couldn't start before four, on account of that busted top, that I had to stow away in the boot. I didn't mean to get sunstroke, so I let her sleep and tried to clean up a little, so I would leave the church about the way I found it, except for a few busted locks and this and that. Getting the car out was a little harder than getting it in. I had to make little dirt run-ways up the steps, soak them with water, and let them bake in the sun, so I could get a little traction for the wheels in reverse. Then I had to tote all the stuff out and load it again, but I had more time, and made a better job of it. When she came out of her siesta, we started off. The arroyo was still a stream, but it was clear water now, and not running deep, so we got across all right.

When we got to Acapulco she steered me around to the hotel where we were going to stop. I don't know if you ever saw a hotel for Mexicans. It was a honey. It was just off the road that skirts the harbor, on the edge of the town, and it was just an adobe barracks, one story high, built around a dirt patio, or court, or whatever you'd call it, and that was all. In each room was a square oil can, what they use to carry water in all over Mexico, and that was the furnishings. You used that to carry your water in, from the well outside, and there wasn't anything else in there at all. Your mat, that you slept on, you were supposed to have with you, and unroll it on the dirt floor yourself. That was why she had been packing all those mats around. Your bedclothes you were supposed to have with you too, except that a Mexican doesn't need bedclothes. He flops as is. The plumbing was al fresco exterior, just over from the well. In the patio was a flock of burros, tied, that the guests had come on, and we parked our car there, and she took her hatbox, the cape, the *espada*, and the ear, and the *hostelero* showed us our room. It was No. 16, and had a fine view of a Mexican with his pants down, relieving his bowels.

"Well, how do you feel?"

"Very nice, *gracias*."

"The heat hasn't got you?"

"No, no. Nicer than Mexico."

"Well, I tell you what. It's too early to eat yet. I think I'll have my suit pressed, then take a walk around and kind of get the lay of the land. Then after sundown, when it's cooler, we'll find a nice place and eat. Yes?"

"Very nice. I look at house."

"All right, but I got ideas on the location."

"Oh, the *político* already have house."

"I see. I didn't know that. All right, then, you see the *político*, have a look at the house, and then we'll eat."

"Yes."

I found a *sastrería*, and sat there while they pressed my suit, but I didn't waste any time on the lay of the land after that. You think I was going to bookkeep for a whorehouse now? A fat chance. Those high notes down the arroyo made everything different. There was a freighter laying out there in the harbor, and I meant to dig out of there, if there was any way in God's world I could promote passage on her.

It was nearly dark before I found the captain. He was having dinner at the Hotel de Mexico, out under the canopy. He was a black Irishman, named Conners, about fifty, with brows that met over his nose, a face the color of a meerschaum pipe, and blistered sunburned hands that were thin and long like a blackjack dealer's. He gave me a fine welcome when I sat down at his table. "My friend, I don't know your uncle in New York, your brother in Sydney, or your sister-in-law back in Dublin, God bless her, nevertheless. I'm not a member of the Ancient, Free, and Accepted Order of Masons, and I don't care if you ever get the twenty pesos to take you to Mexico City. I'll not buy you a drink. Here's a peso to be off, and if you don't mind I'll be having my dinner."

I let the peso lay and didn't move. When he had to look at me again I recited it back to him just like he had handed it to me. "I have no uncle in New York, no brother in Sydney, no sister-in-law in Dublin, thanks for the benediction, nevertheless. I'm not a member of the Ancient, Free, and Accepted Order of Masons, and I'm not on my way to Mexico City. I don't want your drink, and I don't want your peso."

"By your looks, you want something. What is it?"

"I want passage north, if that's where you're headed."

"I'm headed for San Pedro, and the passage will be two hundred and fifteen pesos, cash of the Republic, payable in advance, and entitling you to a fine deck stateroom, three meals a day, and the courtesies of the ship."

"I offer five."

"Declined."

I picked up his peso. "Six."

"Declined."

"I offer sweat. I'll do any reasonable thing to work this

passage out, from swabbing decks to cleaning brass. I'm a pretty fair cook."

"Declined."

"I offer a recipe for Iguana John Howard Sharp that I have just perfected, a dish that would be an experience for you, and probably improve your disposition."

"'Tis the first sensible thing you have said, but there would be a difficulty getting the iguana. At this season they move up to the hills. Declined."

"I offer six pesos and a promissory note for two hundred and nine. The note I guarantee to redeem."

"Declined."

I watched him eating his fish, and by that time I was beginning to be annoyed. "Listen, maybe you don't get this straight. I intend to haul out of here, and I intend to haul out on your boat. Write up your contracts any way you want. The thing to get through your head is: I'm going."

"You're not. You've taken my peso, so be off."

I lit a cigarette and still sat there. "All right, I'll level it out, and quit the feinting and jabbing. I was a singer, and my voice cracked up. Now it's coming back, see? That means if I ever get out of this hellhole of a country, and get back where the money is, I can cash in. I'm all right. I'm as good as I ever was, maybe better. To hell with the promissory note. I guess that was a little tiresome. I ask you as a favor to haul me up to San Pedro, so I can get on my feet again."

When he looked up, his eyes were smoky with hate. "So you're a singer, then. An American singer. My answer is: It wouldn't be safe for me to take you aboard. Before I was out of the harbor with you I'd drop you into the water to rid the world of you. No! And don't take up any more of my time with it."

"What's the matter with an American singer?"

"I even hate the Pacific Ocean. On the Atlantic side, I can get London, Berlin, and Rome on my wireless. But here what is it? Los Angeles, San Francisco, the blue network, the red network, a castrated eunuch urging me to buy soap—and Victor Herbert!"

"He was an Irishman."

"He was a German."

"You're wrong. He was an Irishman."

"I met him in London when I was a young man, and I talked German with him myself."

"He talked German, through choice, especially when he was with other Irishmen. You see, he wasn't proud of it. He didn't want them to know it. All right, look him up."

"Then he was an Irishman, though I hate to say it.— And George Gershwin! There was an Irishman for you."

"He wrote some music."

"He didn't write one bar of music. Victor Herbert, and George Gershwin, and Jerome Kern, and buy the soap for me schoolboy complexion, and Lawrence Tibbett, singing mush. At Tampico, I got Mozart's Jupiter Symphony, that I suppose you never heard of, coming from Rome. Off Panama, I picked up the Beethoven Seventh, with Beecham conducting it, in London—"

"Listen, never mind Beethoven—"

"Oh, it's never mind Beethoven, is it? You would say that, you soap-agent. He was the greatest composer that ever lived!"

"The hell he was."

"And who was? Walter Donaldson, I suppose."

"Well, we'll see."

There were two or three mariachis around, but the place wasn't full yet, so there was a lull in the screeching. I called a man over, and took his guitar. It was tuned right, for a change. My fingers still had calluses on them, from the job in Mexico City, so I could slide up to the high positions without cutting them. I went into the introduction to the serenade from Don Giovanni, and then I sang it. I didn't do any number, didn't try to get any hand, and the rest of them in there hardly noticed me. I just sang it, half-voice, rattled off the finish on the guitar, and put my hand over the strings.

He was to his tamales by now, and he kept putting them down. Then he called the guitar player over, had a long pow-wow in Spanish, and laid down some paper money. The guitar player touched his hat and went off. The waiter took his plate and he stared hard at the table.

". . . It's a delicate point. I've been a Beethoven enthusiast ever since I was a young man, but I've often wondered to myself if Mozart wasn't the greatest musical genius that ever lived. You might be right, you might be right. I bought his guitar, and I'll take it aboard with me. I'm in with a cargo of blasting powder, and I can't clear till I've signed a million of their damned papers. Be at the dock at midnight sharp. I'll lift my hook shortly after."

I left him, my heels lifting like they had grown wings. Everything said lay low until midnight, and never go back to the hotel. But I hadn't eaten yet, and I couldn't make myself go in a café and sit down alone. Along about nine o'clock I walked on up there.

I no sooner turned in the patio before I could see there was something going on. Two or three oil lamps were stuck around, on stools, and some candles. Our car was still where I had left it, but a big limousine was parked across from it, and the place was full of people. By the limousine was a stocky guy, dark taffy-colored, in an officer's uniform with a star on his shoulder and an automatic on his hip, smoking a cigarette. She was sitting on the running board of our car. In between, maybe a couple of dozen Mexicans were lined up. Some of them seemed to be guests of the hotel, some of them the hired help, and the last one was the *hostelero*. Two soldiers with rifles were searching them. When they got through with the *hostelero* they saw me, came over, they grabbed me, stood me up beside him, and searched me too. I never did like a bum's rush, especially by a couple of gorillas that didn't even have shoes.

When the searching was over, the guy with the star started up the line, jabbering at each one in Spanish. That took quite a while. When he got to me he gave me the same mouthful, but she said something and he stopped. He looked at me sharp, and jerked his thumb for me to stand aside. I don't like a thumb any better than I like a bum's rush.

He fired an order at the soldiers then, and they began going in and out of the rooms. In a minute one of them gave a yell and came running out. The guy with the star went in with them, and they came out with our beans, our eggs, our ground corn, our pots, bowls, charcoal, machetes, everything that had been packed on the car. A woman began to wail and the hostelero began to beg. Nothing doing. The guy with the star and the soldiers grabbed them and hustled them out of the court and up the street. Then he barked something else and waved his hand. The whole mob slunk to their rooms, and you could hear them in there mumbling and some of them moaning. He walked over to her, put his arm around her, and she laughed and they talked in Spanish. Quick work, getting the stolen stuff back, and he wanted appreciation.

She went into No. 16 and came out with the hatbox and the other stuff. He opened the door of the limousine.

"Where you going with that guy?"

I didn't know I was going to say it. My play was to stand there and let her go, but this growl came out of my mouth without my even intending it. She turned around, and her eyes opened wide like she couldn't believe what she heard. "But please, he is político."

"I asked you where you're going with him."

"But yes. You stay here. I come mañana, very early. Then we look at house, yes."

She was talking in a phoney kind of way, but not to fool me. It was to fool him, so I wouldn't get in trouble. She kept staring at me, trying to get me to shut up. I was standing by our car, and he came over and snapped something. She came over and spoke to him in Spanish, and he seemed satisfied. The idea seemed to be that I was an American, and was all mixed up on what it was about. I licked my lips, tried to make myself take it easy, play it safe till I got on that boat. I tried to tell myself she was nothing but an Indian girl, that she didn't mean a thing with me, that if she was going off to spend the night with this cluck it was no more than she had done plenty of times before, that she didn't know any different and it was none of my business anyway. No dice. Maybe if she hadn't looked so pretty out there in the moonlight I might have shut up, but I don't think so. Something had happened back in that church that made me feel she belonged to me. I heard my mouth growl again. "You're not going."

"But he is político—"

"And because he's político, and he's fixed you up with a lousy sailor's whorehouse, he thinks he's going to take part of his graft in trade. He made a mistake. You're not going."

"But—"

He stepped up, then, and shot a rattle at me in Spanish, so close I could feel the spit on my face. We hadn't been talking loud. I was too sore to yell, and Mexicans say it soft. He finished, straightened up, and jerked his thumb at me again, toward the hotel. I let him have it. He went down. I stamped my foot on his hand, grabbed the pistol out of the holster. "Get up."

He didn't move. He was out cold. I looked at the hotel. All you could hear was this mumbling and moaning. They hadn't heard anything at all. I jerked open the car door and shoved her in, hatboxes and all. Then I ran around, threw the pistol on the seat, jumped in and started. I went out of the court in second, and by the time I hit the road I was in high.

I snapped on the lights and gave her the gun. In a few seconds I was in the town, and then I knew what a mistake I had made when I came out of that court, and cut right instead of left. I had to get out of there, and get out of there quick before that guy came to, and I couldn't turn around. I mean literally I couldn't turn around. The street was so narrow, and so choked with burros, pigs, goats, mariachis, and people, that even when you met a car you had to saw by, and a turn was impossible. It was no through street. It went through the town, and then, at the hill, it led up to the big tourist hotel, and that was the end of it. I crawled along now, the sweat coming out on my brow, and got to the bottom of the hill. There was no traffic there, but it was still narrow. I turned right on a side road. I thought I might hit a way, after a block or two, that would lead back where I had come from. I didn't. The street just tapered off into two tracks on an open field, that as far as I could see just wandered up in the hills. I pulled into the field, to turn around. I thought I still might have time to slip back through the town, though it didn't look like even Jess Willard could stay out that long. Then back of me I heard shots, yells, and the screech of a motorcycle siren. It was too late. I was cut off. I doused the lights and bumped over to a grove of coconut palms, where anyway I would be shaded from the moonlight.

I lined up toward the town, so I could see, and tried to think. It all depended on whether I had been noticed, turning off the main street. If I hadn't, I might be able to lay low till the moon went down and they were asleep, then go through the town fast, and be on my way to Mexico City before they even knew I had got away. I tried not to think about the ship.

In a minute or so, the sirens began to screech louder, and three single lights streaked out of town around the harbor. That meant they had no idea I was still around. They thought I was on my way to Mexico, and were out after me. That meant we would be safe here for a little while, maybe the whole night. But where it put me, when I did start up to Mexico, and met those patrols coming back, I hated to think. And Mexico was the only place you could go. There wasn't any other road.

We sat there a long time, and then I knew she was crying. "Why you do this? Why you do this to me?"

"Don't you know? Why I—" I tried to make myself say "I love you," but it stuck in my throat. "I wanted you. I didn't want him to have you."

"That is not true. You go away."

"What makes you say that?"

"You sing now, yes? You sing better anybody in Mexico. You stay in Acapulco, in a house? Why you lie? You go away."

"I never even thought of it."

"Now for me, very bad. No house, no. Maybe he shoot me, yes. I can no work more in Mexico. He is very big político. I—why you do this? Why you do this?"

We sat there some more, and I wondered why I didn't

feel like a heel. She had called it on me all right, and I had certainly busted up her run of luck with plenty to spare. But I didn't feel like a heel. I was in a spot, but my face wasn't red. Then it hit me between the eyes: *I wasn't going to run out on her.*

"Juana."

"Yes?"

"Listen to me now. I've got some things to say."

"Please, say nothing."

"In the first place, you were right when you said I was going away, and I did lie to you. While I was out, pretending to look the town over, I arranged passage to the *Estados Unidos del Norte*, on a boat. I was to leave at twelve o'clock."

"I know you lie, when you go out. Yes."

"All right, I lied. You want to hear the rest?"

She didn't answer for a long time. But you could always tell when something was going on inside of her, because her breath would stop for a two beat, and then go on. She turned her head to me once, and then looked away. "Yes."

"When I went up to the hotel, I intended to take you out to dinner, sit around a while, then drift out to the *caballeros*, and not come back. Then you started off with him, and I knew I wasn't going to let you go, and it wasn't only that I didn't like him. I wanted you myself, and I wasn't going to let him have you, or anybody have you."

"But why?"

"I'll get to that. I'm not done yet. Now I'm going away. I told you I used to be a singer. I used to be a very good singer, one of the best in the world, and I made a lot of money, and I will again. But I can't do anything in Mexico. I'm going back to my own country, the *Estados Unidos del Norte*. Now, here's what I'm getting at. Do you want to come with me?"

"Is that very big country?"

"Much bigger than Mexico."

"How you go?"

"We have the car, and you still have a little money. In a little while, after things quiet down, we'll slip through the town and go as far as we can before daylight. Then tomorrow night, we'll start out again, and with luck we'll make Mexico City. We'll lay low another day, and the next night we'll be in Monterey. One more night and we're at Laredo, and I'll figure a way to get you across. Once we're in my country, we're all right."

"That is impossible."

"Why?"

"They know the auto. They catch us, sure."

I knew that was right, even before she said it. In the United States, once you're across a state line, you could go quite a while without being caught. But down there, the state line doesn't mean much. Those guys with rifles, they're federal troops, and with just a car now and then up that road, there wasn't a chance they would miss us, night time, day time, or any other time. ". . . In bus, perhaps."

"What was that, Juana?"

"Ride little way, hide auto. Then in morning, take bus. Maybe they no catch."

"All right, we'll do that."

"But why? Why you no go alone?"

"All right, now we come to the big why. You like me?"

"Yes, much."

"I like you."

I sat looking at her, wondering why I couldn't go the whole hog, tell her I loved her and be done with it. Then I remembered how many times I had sung those words, in three or four different languages, how phoney they sounded, and how much trouble I had in putting them across. Then it came to me that I hated them, not for what they said, but for what they didn't say. They told it all except what you felt in your bones, your belly, and all those other places. They said you might die for a woman, but missed how hungry you could get for her, just to be near her, just to know she was around. ". . . I could make it stronger than that, Juana. Maybe I don't have to."

"They catch us, sure. They kill us."

"You willing to take a chance?"

It was a long time before she said anything, and before

she did she took my hand and pressed it. Then she looked up, and I knew that whatever it was going to be, there was no fooling around about it. It was the works. . . . "Yes."

A little tingle went over me, but what I said was dumb enough. "Yes, what?"

"What do you mean?"

"Don't you think it's about time for us to pick out something for you to call me? I can't very well keep on being Señor."

"I call you Hoaney."

I half wished she had picked out something different than what she had called every Weehawken slob that had showed up at her crib, but I didn't say anything. Then something caught my throat. It came to me that she wasn't calling me "Honey." She was calling me Johnny—her way. "Kiss me, Juana. That's exactly what I want you to call me."

The town was dark now, and quiet. I started, pulled out of the grove, and got over the road. As soon as I could I went into high, not for speed, but for quiet. With all that stuff out of the car we didn't make much noise, but I cut her back to the slowest roll that was in her, and we crept along until we got to the main street. I stopped, and listened. I didn't hear anything, so I started up again, and turned the corner, to the left. I hadn't put the lights on, and the moon was hanging low over the ocean, so the right side of the main street was in shadow. I had gone half a block when she touched my arm. I rolled in to the curb and stopped. She pointed. About three blocks down the street, on the left, where the moonlight lit him up, was a cop. He was walking away from us. He was the only one in sight. She leaned to me and whispered: "He go, so."

She motioned with her hand, meaning around the corner. That's how I went. I gave him about five seconds, then reached for the starter. The car tilted. Somebody was beside me, on the running board. I still had the gun beside me. I snatched it and turned. A brown face was there, not six inches from mine. Then I saw it was Conners.

"Is that you, lad?"

"Yes. God, you gave me a start."

"Where've you been? I've been looking all over for you! I've broken out my hook, I'm ready to go, I'm out of humor with you."

"I got in some trouble."

". . . Don't tell me it was you that hit the general?"

"I did."

His eyes popped open and he began to talk in a whisper. "The penalty is death, lad, the penalty is death."

"Irregardless of that—"

"Not so loud. It's all over town. One of them could be sleeping, and if they hear the English, they'll yell and it'll be the end of you. . . . Did you mind what I said? The penalty is death. He'll take you to the jail and they'll spend an hour booking you, filling out every paper they've got. Then he'll take you out and have them shoot you—for trying to escape."

"If they catch me."

"They'll catch you. For God's sake, come on."

"I'm not coming."

"Did you hear me? The penalty—"

"Since I saw you, there are two of us. Miss Montes, Capitán Conners."

"I'm happy to know you, Miss Montes."

"Gracias, Capitán Conners."

He treated her like a princess, and she acted like one. But then he leaned close and put it in my ear. "You can't do it, man. You can't take up with some girl you met tonight, and you'll be putting her in terrible danger, too. She's a pretty little thing, but hark what I'm telling you. You must come on."

"I didn't just meet her tonight, and she's with me."

He looked up and down the street, and then at his watch. Then looked at me hard. "Lad—do you know the Leporello song?"

"I do."

"Then come on, the pair of you."

He slipped around the car and helped her out. She had the hatbox in her lap. He took it. She carried the other stuff. I grabbed the door, for fear he would slam it mechanically. He didn't. I slipped out on the right side, after her. He pulled us back of the car. "We'll keep the automobile between us and that policeman, down the street."

We tiptoed back to the corner I had just turned, and instead of going the way I had, he pulled us the other way, toward the beach. We came to a crooked alley, and turned into that.

Two minutes after that we trotted out on a dock, and dropped into a launch. Two minutes after that, we were on the deck of the *Port of Cobh*, with beer and sandwiches coming up. Two minutes after that we were slipping past the headland, and I was cocked back with a guitar on my knee, rolling the Leporello song out for him, and she was pouring beer.

6

IT WAS A HAPPY WEEK, all right. I didn't sing much, except a little at night, if he wanted it. Most of the time we sat around and fanned about music. She would be with us, and then she wouldn't be. He gave us the royal suite, and the main feature was a shower bath, with sea water coming out of it. It was the first time she had been under one. Maybe it was the first time she ever had a bath, I don't know. Mexicans are the cleanest people on earth. Their face is clean, their feet are clean, their clothes are clean, and they don't stink. But when they bathe, or whether they bathe, I can't tell you. To her it was a new toy, and every time I'd go looking for her I'd find her in there, stripped clean, under the water. I guess I generally hung around. She was something for a sculptor to hire, and she had just enough of the copper in her to make her look like something poured from metal, especially with the water shining on her shoulders. I didn't let her see me look, at first, but then I found out she liked it. She'd stand on her toes, and stretch her arms, and let her muscles ripple, and then laugh. So of course that led to this and that.

The second night out, he got off on a harangue against Verdi, Puccini, Mascagni, Bellini, Donizetti, and "that most unspeakable wop of all, Rossini." That was where I stopped him. "Hold on, hold on, hold on. On those others, I haven't got much to say. I sing them, but I don't talk about them, though Donizetti is a lot better than most people think. But on Rossini, you're crazy."

"The William Tell Overture is the worst piece of music ever written."

"There's music in it, but it's not his best."

"There's no music in it of any kind."

"Well, how's this?"

I picked up the guitar and gave him a little of Semiramide. You can't play a Rossini crescendo on a guitar, but I did what I could. He listened, his face set like flint. I finished and was going to start something else, when he touched my arm. "Play a little of that again."

I played it again, then gave him some Italians in Algiers, and then some Barber. It took quite a while. I know a lot of Rossini. I didn't sing, just played. On the woodwind strain in the Barber overture, I just brushed the strings with my fingers, then for the climax came in big over the hole, and it really sounded like something. I stopped, and he smoked his pipe a long time. " 'Tis fine, musicianly music, isn't it?"

"It's all of that. And it's no worse for being gay, and not taking itself too seriously."

"Aye, it has a twinkle in its eye, and a sparkle in its beat."

"Your friend Beethoven patronized him, the son-of-a-bitch. Told him to keep on writing tunes, that was what he was good for. All Rossini was doing at the time was trying to give him a lift, so he wouldn't have to live like a hog in the dump he found him in."

"If he patronized him it was his right."

"The hell it was. When a Beethoven overture is as good as a Rossini overture, then it'll be his right. Until then, let him keep his goddam mouth shut."

"Lad, lad, you're profaning a temple."

"No, I'm not. You say he's the greatest composer that ever lived, and so do I. He wrote the nine greatest symphonies ever put on paper, and that makes him the greatest composer. But listen, symphonies are not all of music. When you get to the overtures, Beethoven's name is not at the top, and Rossini's is. The idea of a man that could write a thing like the Leonora No. 3 high-hatting Rossini. Why, when those horns sound off, off-stage, it's a cheap vaudeville effect that makes the William Tell Overture sound like a Meistersinger's Prelude, by comparison."

"I confess I don't like it."

"Oh yeah, he would show the boys how to write an overture, wouldn't he? He didn't have overtures in him. You know why? To write an overture, you've got to love the theatre, and he didn't. Did you ever hear Fidelio?"

"I have, and it shames me—"

"But Rossini loved the theatre, and that's why he could write an overture. He takes you into the theatre,— hell, you can even feel them getting into their seats, and smell the theatre smell, and see the lights go up on the curtain. Who the hell told Beethoven he could treat that guy as somebody with an amusing talent that he ought to cultivate?"

"Just the same he was a great man."

I played the minuet from the Eighth Symphony. You can get most of that on the guitar. ". . . That was something to hear. By the way you play him, lad, you think he's a great man yourself, I take it?"

"Yes."

"The other too. From now on I shall listen to him." We were several days out before he got around to Mc-Cormack, and he kind of brought it up offhand, as we were sitting on deck at sundown, like it was just something he happened to think of. But when he found out I thought McCormack was one of the greatest singers that ever lived, he began to talk. "So you say the singers admire the fellow?"

"Admire him? Does a ballplayer admire Ty Cobb?"

"Between ourselves, I'm no enthusiast for the art. As you've observed, I'm a symphony man myself, and I believe the great music of the world has been written for fiddlers, not singers. But with McCormack I make an exception. Not because he's an Irishman, I give you my word on that. You were right about Herbert. If there's one thing an Irishman hates more than a landlord it's another Irishman. 'Tis because he makes me feel music I had previously been indifferent to. I don't speak of the ballads he sings, mush a man wouldn't spit into. But I have heard him sing Händel. I heard him sing a whole program of Händel at a private engagement in Boston."

"He can sing it, all right."

"Until then, I had not cared for Händel, but he revealed it to me. 'Tis something to be grateful for, the awakening to Händel. What is the reason for that? I've heard a million of your Wops, Frogs and Yankees sing Händel, aye and plenty of Englishmen, but not one of them can sing it the way that fellow can."

"Well, in the first place, he's good. That's something you can't quite cut up into pieces and measure off. And when a man's good, he's generally good all the way down the line. McCormack has music in him, so he no sooner opens his trap than there's a tingle to it, no matter what he sings. He has an instinct for style that never lets him down. He never drags an andante too slow, or hustles an allegro too fast. He never turns a dumb phrase, or forces, or misgauges a climax. When he does it, it's always right, with a big R. What he did for Händel was to bring it to life for you. Up to then, you probably thought it was pale, thin, tinkle-tankle stuff—"

"To my shame I did."

"And then he stepped into it, like a bugler at dawn—"

"That's it, that's it, like a bugler at dawn. You can't imagine what it was like, lad. He stood there, the most arrogant figure of a man I ever saw, with his chest thrown out and his head thrown back, and his thumbs in his little black book of words, like a cardinal starting the mass. And without a word, he began to sing. And the sun came up, and the sun came up."

"And in the second place—"

"Yes, lad, in the second place?"

"He had a great voice."

"He could have the Magic Flute in his throat and I'd never know it."

"Well, he goddam near *had* the Magic Flute in his throat, if somebody happened to ask you. And your ears knew it, even if your head didn't. He had a great voice, not just a good voice. I don't mean big. It was never big, though it was big enough. But what makes a great voice is beauty, not size, and beauty will get you, I don't care if it's in a man's throat or a woman's leg."

"You may be right. I hadn't thought of it."

"And in the third place—"

"Go on, 'tis instructive to me."

"—There's the language he was born to. John McCormack comes from Dublin."

"He does not. He comes from Athlone."

"Didn't he live in Dublin?"

"No matter. They speak a fine brogue in Athlone, almost as fine as in Belfast."

"It's a fine brogue, but it's not a brogue. It's the English language as it was spoken before all the other countries of the world forgot how to speak it. There's two things a singer can't buy, beg or steal, and that no teacher, coach or conductor can give him. One is his voice, the other is the language that was born in his mouth. When McCormack was singing Händel he was singing English, and he sings it as no American and no Englishman will ever sing English. But not like an Irishman. Not with all that warmth, color, and richness that McCormack puts into it."

" 'Tis pleasant to hear you say that."

"You speak a fine brogue yourself."

"I try to say what I mean."

We were creeping past Ensenada, four or five miles out,

and we smoked a while without saying anything. The sea was like glass, but you could see the hotel in the setting sun, and the white line of surf around the harbor. We smoked a while, but I'm a bit of a bug on that subject of language, and what a man brings on stage with him besides what he was taught. I started up again, and told him how all the great Italian singers have come from the city of Naples, and gave him a few examples of singers with fine voices that never made the grade because they were bums, and people won't listen to bums. About that, I knew plenty. Then I got off on Mexico, and about that, I guess you can realize I was pretty bitter. I began getting it off my chest. He listened, but pretty soon he stopped me. "Not so fast, lad, not so fast. 'Tis instructive that Caruso came from Naples, as McCormack came from Athlone, and that it was part of his gift, but when you speak so of Mexico, I take exception."

"I say they can't sing because they can't talk."

"They talk soft."

"They talk soft, but they talk on top of their throats—and they've got nothing to say! Listen, you can't spend a third of your life on the dirt floor of an adobe hut, and then expect people to listen to you when you stand up and try to sing Mozart. Why, sit down, you goddam Indian, and—"

"I'm losing patience with you."

"Did you ever hear them sing?"

"I don't know if they can sing, and I don't care. But they're a great people."

"At what? Is there one thing they do well?"

"Life is not all doing. It's part being. They're a great people. The little one in there—"

"She's an exception."

"She's not. She's a typical Mexican, and I should know one when I see her by now. I've been sailing these coasts for fifty years. She speaks soft, and holds herself like the little queen that she is. There's beauty in her."

"I told you, she's an exception."

"There's beauty in them."

"Sure, the whole goddam country is a musical comedy

71

set, if that's what you mean. But when you get past the scenery and the costumes, what then? Under the surface what do you find? Nothing!"

"I don't know what I find. I'm no great hand at words, and it would be hard for me to say what I find. But I find *something*. And I know this much: if it's beauty I feel, then it must be under the surface, because beauty is always under the surface."

"Under the bedrock, in that hellhole."

"I think much about beauty, sitting alone at night, listening to my wireless, and trying to get the reason of it, and understand how a man like Strauss can put the worst sounds on the surface that ever profaned the night, and yet give me something I can sink my teeth into. This much I know: True beauty has terror in it. Now I shall reply to your contemptuous words about Beethoven. He has terror in him, and your overture writers have not. Fine music they wrote, and after your remarks I shall listen to them with respect. But you can drop a stone into Beethoven, and you will never hear it strike bottom. The eternities and the infinities are in it, and they strike at the soul, like death. You mind what I'm telling you, there is terror in the little one too, and I hope you never forget it in your relations with her."

There wasn't much I could say to that. I had felt the terror in her, God knows. We lit up again, and watched Ensenada turn gray, blue and violet. My cigarettes were all gone by then, and I was smoking his tobacco, and one of his pipes, that he had cleaned out for me on a steam jet in the boiler. Not a hundred feet from the ship a black fin lifted out of the water. It was an ugly thing to see. It was at least thirty inches high, and it didn't zigzag, or cut a V in the water, or any of the things it does in books. It just came up and stayed a few seconds. Then there was the swash of a big tail and it went down.

"Did you see it, lad?"

"God, it was an awful-looking thing, wasn't it?"

"It cleared up for me what I've been trying to say to you. Sit here, now, and look. The water, the surf, the colors on the shore. You think they make the beauty of the tropical sea, aye, lad? They do not. 'Tis the knowledge of what lurks below the surface of it, that awful-looking thing, as you call it, that carries death with every move that it makes. So it is, so it is with all beauty. So it is with Mexico. I hope you never forget it."

We docked at San Pedro around three in the afternoon, and all I had to do was walk ashore. He gave me dollars for our pesos, so I wouldn't have any trouble over that part, and came down the plank with me. It took about three seconds. I was an American citizen, I had my passport, they looked at it, and that was all. I had no baggage. But she was different, and how she was going to get ashore was making me pretty nervous. He had her below decks, under cover, and so far so good, but that didn't mean she was in, by a long way. He didn't seem much upset, though. He walked through the pier with me, waving at his friends, stopping to introduce me to his broker, taking it easy. When he got to the loading platform outside, he stood there and lit a cigar his broker had given him. "Across there is a little cove they call Fish Harbor. It is reached by a ferry, and you should find out how to get there this afternoon, but don't arrive before dark, as you should not be seen hanging around. By the wharves runs a street, and on the main thoroughfare leading down to it is a little Japanese restaurant, about a stone's throw from the water. Be there at nine o'clock, sharp. Order beer, and drink it slowly till I come."

He clapped me on the shoulder, and went back to the ship. I walked down and found how the ferry ran. Then I went in a lunchroom and had something to eat. Then I went in a moving picture, so I could sit down. I don't even know what the show was. Every fifteen or twenty minutes I would go out in the lobby to look at the clock. Whatever it was, I saw it twice. Around seven I left the theatre and walked down to the ferry. It was quite a while coming, but just about dark it showed up and I went across. It took about ten minutes. I walked down to Fish Harbor, found it without having to ask anybody about it, and then spotted the restaurant. I walked past it, then found a clock and checked on the time. It was half past eight. I walked on to where the street turned into a road, and kept on going until I figured I had covered three quarters of a mile. Then I turned around and came back. When I passed the clock it said five minutes to nine.

I went in and ordered beer. There were five or six guys in there, fishermen by their looks, and I raised my glass at them, and they raised back. I didn't want to act like some mysterious stranger, looking neither right nor left. After that they paid no attention to me. At ten after he came in. He shook hands all around in a big way, then sat down with me, and ordered beer. They seemed to know him. When his beer came, he sent the Jap out for a cab, and then began telling me, and telling them, about this trouble he had on his ship. He had his things packed, and was already to come ashore, when a launch showed up out of the night, and began yelling up at the pier for somebody named Charlie. "They kept it up, until I got so sick of Charlie I could have thrown a pin at them."

He was pretty funny, but I wasn't in the humor for it. They were, though. "Who was Charlie?"

"I never did find out. But wait a minute. Of course my second officer had his face out the hatch, ogling the girls, and do you know what the young upstart did? He called out: 'Forget about Charlie! Come aboard, girls. I'll give you a hand through the hatch—and let a real man take care of you!' And before I knew it he had a line down, they had made the launch fast, and they were aboard my ship!"

"What did you do?"

"I was down there in a flash and I ordered them off! Off and begone!' I said to them. 'Out of the hatch where you came in, and let me see no more of you!'"

"Did they go?"

"They did not! They stood laughing at me, and invited me to go with them! Then the man that was with them seconded the invitation, and my second officer had the effrontery to second him. I was so furious I could not trust myself to speak. But then with an effort, I got myself under control, and I said to him: ''Tis an official matter,' I reminded him, 'to be entered on your papers

74

and reported to your owners. Get these girls out of here, and at once.' Do you know what those girls said to me?"

"What they say?"

" 'Nuts.' "

That got a laugh. "I argued with them. I pleaded with them, as I didn't want any trouble. At last I had to appeal to the guard on the pier, who was standing there, looking down into the hatch, listening to it. 'Is that right, my man?' I said to him, 'that such entry into a ship is in violation of law? That they must enter by the plank, and pass the guard, otherwise be subject to arrest?"

" 'It is, captain,' he said, 'and they'll not pass the guard if I have anything to do with it.' "

"That seemed to frighten them, and out they went, the girls, the man and my second officer. Him I will deal with in the morning. But what I cannot understand about these American girls is the boldness of them. Not one of them could have been more than nineteen, and where were their mothers all that time? What were they doing in that launch at all? Will you tell me that?"

They all chimed in with what a tough bunch the young girls are nowadays, and then the Jap came in and said the cab was ready. He paid, and we took the valise he had brought with him, and went out and put it in the cab, and he told the driver to wait. Then he started to walk down toward the wharves. "Well, what about her?"

He didn't seem to hear me. " 'Twas a noisy ten minutes. Of course, if the guard on the pier had been observant, he would have noticed that the man in the launch was my first officer. He would also have noticed that whereas three young girls came into the hatch, four of them went out of it."

"Oh."

We got to the wharves, strolled out on one, then strolled back, and stood on the corner, smoking. Out in the basin somewhere a launch started up. In a minute or two it slipped in to the wharf, stopped a second, and she hopped ashore and came running to us. Then it shoved off and disappeared. I had wanted to go down and thank those guys for all they had done for us, but he wouldn't

75

let me. "I'll tell them all you say. The three girls they found have no idea what they've been a party to, and the less they know, the less they have to tell. They will see a nice picture show, now, and that's enough."

It was always catching me by surprise, how glad I was to be with her, and I got this catch in my throat when she came running up to us, laughing like it had all been a big joke. We walked back to the cab, got in, and told the driver to take the ferry and go to the nearest Los Angeles bus stop. She sat in the middle and I took her hand. He looked out the window. She turned to him, but he kept staring at the buildings going by. Then she reached out and took his hand. He came out of it on that. He took her hand in both of his, and patted it, but it was a minute or two before he said anything. ". . . There's something I'd like to say to both of you. I've enjoyed every minute of your stay on my ship. I wish you all happiness, and as you're in love, you may have it. 'Tis a big world, and I bob around it like a cork in a tub. But should you ever need me, and should I be there, you have only to say the word. Only to say the word."

". . . Gracias, Señor Capitán.—. . . This big world, I go around, too . . . But, you need me—you say word, say word only."

"Me too."

". . . 'Tis a pretty night."

On the ferry the driver went forward to have a smoke, and we were alone. He sat up and began to talk. "Her things are all in the valise. It holds them better than her own little box, especially that sword that she carries with her. She's wearing no hat, and it would be a good idea if you were to stow your own hat with her stuff. You're both well burned by the sun, and without hats you could well be a couple that has spent a day at the beach, and arouse no suspicion that you're just off a boat."

I opened the valise, put my hat in it, and he went on. "Inquire of the busman, and get off as near what they call the Plaza as you can. In that neighborhood are many small hotels catering to Mexicans of the town, and you will attract no attention. Register as Mr. and Mrs. Perhaps you will not believe it, but under American laws you must write it so, and so long as you do, they will not care. In the morning, get up very early, and as soon as you can, get a hat on her. I have packed all her shawls, and forbidden her to carry one, as they will betray her sooner than anything else. I doubt if she has ever had a hat on in her life, so be careful that you pick one yourself, a little hat exactly like all the other hats in the place. When you have bought the hat, buy her a little dress. I know nothing of girls' clothes myself, but her little things make me think of Mexico, and sharper eyes than mine might become suspicious. Buy her a dress like every other dress in the place. When you have bought her a hat and bought her a dress, you can breathe easier about illegal entry. Her accent will attract no attention. In America are as many accents as the countries of the world, and she could have lived here all her life and still speak as she does. But the clothes will mark her. She should meet few Mexicans. There is a belief among them that the United States government pays informers against immigrants of her kind. It does not, but one of them might turn her in for the sake of the legendary reward. As soon as you can, get work. A working man is his own answer to all questions, an idle man is a riddle they all try to guess. It would be a good idea if she learned to read and write."

We got out at the bus stop, and shook hands, and then she put her arms around him and kissed him. He was shaken up as I stepped over to help him into the cab. "And you'll mind what I've been telling you, lad?—about her, and Mexico, and all the rest of it?"

"I'll mind. For the rest of my life."

"See that you do. For the rest of your life."

7

WE FOUND A LITTLE HOTEL, a two-dollar joint on Spring Street, and didn't have any trouble. It was about what you would expect, but after Mexico it was like a palace, and they gave us a room with a shower, so she was happy. After she had splashed enough water to suit her, she came and lay in my arms, and I lay there thinking about how we were starting our life together in my own country, and wanted to say something about it, but next thing I knew she was asleep. We got up early the next morning, and as soon as the stores were open, went out to get that hat. Then we got a dress and a light coat. The hat was $1.95, the dress $3.79, and the coat $6. That left us $38 out of her 500 pesos. We stopped by a little restaurant, had a little breakfast, and then I took her back to the hotel and went out to find work.

First thing I did was wire my agent in New York, the one that had sent me down to Mexico. I told her I was all right again, and to see what she could do, as I wanted to get going. Then I bought a Variety, the Hollywood edition, and looked in there to see if any agents carried ads. Quite a few of them did, and the one that seemed to be what I wanted was named Stoessel, and had offices in Hollywood, so I got on a bus and went out there. It took me an hour to get in to see him, and he never even bothered to look at me. "Brother, out here singers are a drug on the market, and they've quit fooling with them. They've had them all, and how many come through? Eddy, MacDonald, Pons, Martini, and Moore—and even Pons and Martini ain't so hot. The rest of them, flops, nothing but flops. And it ain't only that they flop, they have a hell of a time getting stories for them. They're through with singers. When they want a singer, little production number maybe, they know where to get him. Outside of that—out. I'm sorry, but you're in the wrong place."

"I didn't mean pictures. How about theatres?"

"I could book you twelve weeks straight, right up the coast, book you in a minute, if you was a name. Without a name for the marquee, you ain't worth a dime."

"I'm fairly well known."

"I never heard of no John Howard Sharp."

"I sang mainly in Europe."

"This ain't Europe."

"How about night clubs?"

"I don't fool with that small stuff. You want to go on in a night club, there's plenty of them around. If that interests you, you might pick up quite a little time here and there, this and that. Try Fanchon and Marco. Maybe they got a spot for you."

I walked down on Sunset, to Fanchon and Marco. They were putting up a dance act, and a singer didn't seem to fit. I went in a radio station. They gave me an audition, and said they'd let me have some sustaining time in the afternoon, but they wouldn't pay for it, and I'd have to bring my own accompanist. I said I'd be back.

Around four o'clock I went in a night club on La Brea, and they let me sing for them, and then said they'd put me on, $7.50 a night, tips and meals, report in evening clothes at nine o'clock. I said I'd let them know. I found a costume place to go in and rent an evening outfit. The price was $3 a night, $10 by the week, and that would leave a little profit, but they had nothing in there that would fit. I'm six feet, and weighed nearly two hundred, and that's an out size for a costume place. I went back to Spring Street. There was a little place still open, and I went in and bought a second-hand guitar for $5. I wasn't going to pay an accompanist to get me on the air. With that guitar, I could do my own accompanying.

I kept that up three or four days. I parked the guitar in the radio station, and went in there every day at two thirty. I was to get fifteen minutes, and be announced

79

under my name, but when I cut myself up into two pieces, John Howard Sharp, baritone, and Signor Giuseppe Bondo, the eminent Italian guitar player, they gave me a half hour. I'd sing a couple of numbers, and then I'd introduce the Signor, and the Signor would announce his selections in a high voice, in Italian. Then I'd try to translate, and get it all wrong, so if I said it was to be Hearts and Flowers, the Signor would play Liebestraum, or something like that. The station manager thought that was a pretty good gag, and made us a regular feature, and put our names in the paper. After the second day he got twenty or thirty letters about me, and two or three hundred about the Signor, and he got all excited and said he was going to find a sponsor for us. A sponsor, it turned out, was an advertiser that would pay us.

One of those days, after the broadcast, I took the guitar out with me and went to Griffith Park, where the Iowa Society was having a picnic, forty or fifty thousand of them. I thought if I went singing around, there might be some tips. I had never taken a tip, and I wondered how I was going to feel about it. I needn't have worried. The Iowa Society liked me fine, but none of them dug into their pocket. But next day I went in the Biltmore, where the Rotary Club was having lunch. I marched right in with the guitar, just like I was supposed to be there, and when I got into the dining-room I went to the center of the U table that they were all sitting around, hit a chord and started to sing. I picked the Trumpeter, because you can rip into it right from the start without any waiting around for a chorus to get started on. A captain and three waiters hustled over to throw me out, but two or three of them yelled, "Let him alone! Let him alone!"

I got a hand, and piled a couple of numbers on top of it. I remember one of them was the Speaks Mandalay. Then some egg up in the corner began to yell "Pollyochy! Pollyochy!" I didn't think it was a Pagliacci crowd, so I didn't pay any attention to him, but he kept it up, and then some of the others yelled "Pollyochy!" too, mostly to shut him up. So I whammed into the introduction, and began singing the Prologue. It's not my favorite piece of music, but I do it all right, and at the end of the andante I gave them plenty of A flat. By rights, you sing A flats for dough, and for nothing else, but it had been a long time since anybody wanted to hear mine. I swelled it and cut, and then on the E flat that follows it I shook the windows. When I finished I got a big hand, and gave them some Trovatore and Traviata.

When it was time for the speeches the president, or chairman, or whatever he was, called me up, and told me to wait, and they began making up a pot for me. They borrowed a tray from a waiter and passed it around and when it came back it was full of silver. He handed it to me, and I thanked him, and dumped it in my pocket. I had taken a tip, but I didn't feel anything. I went out in the washroom to count it.

It was $6.75, but we were getting low, getting low. Even with that, we were down to $22, and nobody showing the least interest in John Howard Sharp. Still, there was an outdoor performance of Carmen that night at the Hollywood Bowl, at a dollar and a half top but with some seats at seventy-five cents, so of course we had to go. If you want to know where to find an opera singer the night some opera is being given you'll find him right there, and no other place. A baseball player, for some reason, prefers a ball game.

So I told her to get dressed, so we could eat early, and try to get out there in time to get some kind of decent seat. By that time she had quit playing with the shower bath to play with the hat. She'd put it on, and take it off, and put it on again, and look at herself in the mirror, and ask if she had it on right, then take it off and start all over again. I generally said it looked swell, but it was funny how dumb she was, catching on to how it worked. Up to then, I had always thought of a woman's hat as something that she put on, and forgot about, and that was that. But the way she did it, it was the funniest-looking thing you ever saw in your life. Half the time she would get it on backwards, and even when she didn't, she would pull it down on her head some way that made it look like it didn't even belong to her. I tried the best I

81

could and it was better than her way, but it always looked like a man's necktie would if somebody else tied it for him.

It was a warm night, so she wasn't wearing the coat. She decided to wear the bullfighter's cape. It looked pretty swell, so it was all right with me. When she had laid it out, she came over for me to put the finishing touches on the hat. I fixed it so it looked almost right, and then she went over to the mirror to have a look. She gave it one last pull that made it all wrong, put on the cape, and turned around to be admired. "Am I very pretty?"

"You're the prettiest thing in the world."

"Yes."

The curtain was advertised at eight thirty, and we got there at seven thirty, but I found out I didn't even know what early meant on a night when they're giving opera in the Hollywood Bowl. Most of those people, I think, had been there since breakfast. The best we could get was up on the rim, at least a quarter of a mile from the show. It was the first time I had ever seen the Hollywood Bowl, and maybe you've never been in it. It's so big you can't believe it. It was just about dark when we got there, and they were pouring into it through every ramp, and everywhere you looked there were people. I counted the house as well as I could, and by my figuring when they all got in there would be twenty thousand of them. As it turned out, that was about right. I sat there wondering whether they used amplifiers or what the hell they did. It frightened you to think of singing in such a place.

I looked on the program to see who was singing. I had heard of a couple of them. The José and the Micaela were second-line Metropolitan people. There was a program note on the Carmen. She was a local girl. I knew the Escamillo. He was a wop named Sabini that sang Silvio in Palermo one night when I was singing Tonio. I hadn't heard of him in five years. The rest of them I didn't know.

They played the introduction and the lights went up and we began to have a good time. I'm telling you, that was opera that you dream about. They didn't have any curtain. They put the lights up, and there it was, and when they finished they blacked out and came up with a baby spot for the bows. The orchestra was down front. Beyond was a low flight of wide steps, and quite a way beyond that was the stage, without the shell they use for concerts. On that they built a whole town, the guardhouse on one side, cafés on the other, the cigarette factory in back. You had to rub your eyes to believe you weren't in Spain. The way they lit it was great. They've got a light box in that Bowl that tops anything I ever saw. And that stage town was just filled with people. The performance seemed to be given with some kind of hook-up between a ballet school and some local chorus, and they must have had at least three hundred out there. When the bell rang and the girls began pouring out of the factory, they poured out. It was really lunch time. Between acts, they rolled that stuff off, and rolled on the café for the second act, and the rocks for the third act, and the bullring entrance for the fourth act. The place is so big that with the lights down nobody paid any attention to what they were doing out there. They didn't use any amplifiers. Big as it was, the acoustics were so perfect you could hear every whisper. That was the thing I couldn't get over.

The principals were just fair, maybe not as good as that, except for the two from the Met, but I didn't mind. They were giving a performance, and that's enough. So when this little thing happened, I didn't pay any attention to it. A singer can spot trouble a mile away, but I was there for a good time, so what the hell? But then I woke up.

What happened was that in the middle of the scene in the first act, where the soldiers bring Carmen out from the factory after she's cuffed another girl around, a chorister in a uniform stepped up to the Zuniga, jerked his thumb backstage, and began to sing the part. The Zuniga walked off. That was all. They did it so casually that it almost seemed like part of the opera, and I don't think twenty people out there thought anything of it. You would have had to know the opera to have spotted it. I wondered about it, because the Zuniga had a pretty good bass voice, and he had been doing all right. But I was listening to the Carmen, and she started the Seguidilla before I tumbled to what was up.

I jumped up, grabbed the bullfighter cape off her, whipped off my own coat and put it on her, and pointed down the hill. "Meet me after it's over! You understand?"

"Where you go?"

"Never mind. Meet me there. You got it?"

"Yes."

I skipped around the rim, took the ramp on the run, ducked back of the stage, and asked a stagehand for the manager. He pointed to some cars that were parked out back. I went back there, and sure enough, there was the Zuniga, still in his captain's uniform, and a fat guy, standing by a car and arguing with somebody inside. I tapped the fat guy on the shoulder. He batted at me with his hand and didn't even look. "I'm busy. See me later."

"Goddamn it, I'm singing your Escamillo for you!"

"Get the hell away!"

"What's the matter with you—are you snowed in? You called this guy off to get dressed—*and he can't sing it!*"

The Zuniga turned around. "You heard him, Morris. I can't sing F's. I can't do it."

"I've heard you do it."

"Transposed, yes."

"They'll set it down for you!"

"How? They can't rescore a whole number between acts! They got no parts to set it down *with!*"

"For Christ sake! They can read it down—"

"They can like hell. It's out!"

About that time, the man in the car put his head out, and it was Sabini. When he saw me he grabbed me and began kissing me with one side of his mouth and selling me to the manager with the other. Then he began giving me an earful of Italian, a mile a minute, explaining to me he didn't dare get out of his car, didn't even dare be seen, or his wife's process servers would get him, and that was why he couldn't sing. Then he did get out, on the far side, lifted a trunk out of the rumble, and called me around. He began stripping me, and as fast as he got one piece off me, he'd have a piece of the Toreador costume out of the trunk for me to put on. The manager lit a cigarette and stood there watching us. Then he went off. "It's up to the conductor."

There was a big roar from the Bowl that meant the first act was over. Sabini jumped in the car and snapped on the lights. I sat down in front of them and the Zuniga took the make-up kit and began making me up. He stuck on the coleta and I tried the hat. It fit. When the manager came back he had a young guy with him in evening clothes, the conductor. I got up and spoke. He looked me over. "You've sung Escamilla?"

"At least a hundred times."

"Where?"

"Paris, among other places. And not at the Opera. At the Comique, if that means anything to you."

"What name did you sing under?"

"In Italy, Giovanni Sciaparelli. In France and Germany my own, John Howard Sharp."

He gave me a look that would have curdled milk, turned his back, and beckoned to the Zuniga.

"Hey, what's the matter?"

"Yes, I've heard of you. And you're washed up."

I cut one loose they must have heard in Glendale.

"Does that sound like I'm washed up? Does it?"

"You lost your voice."

"Yeah, and I got it back."

He kept looking at me, opened his mouth once or twice to say something, then shook his head and turned to the manager. "It's no use, Morris. He can't do it. I just happened to think of that last act. . . . Mr. Sharp, I wish I could use you. It would pull us out of a spot. But for the sake of the ballet school, we've interpolated Arlésienne music into Act IV, and I've scored the baritone into it, and—"

"Oh, Arlésienne, hey? Listen: Cue me in. That's all I ask. Just cue me in!"

You think that's impossible, that a man can go on and sing stuff he never even saw? All right, once there was an

85

old Aborn baritone that's dead now, by the name of Harry Luckstone, brother of Isidore Luckstone, the singing teacher. He had a cousin named Henry Myers, that writes a little music now and then. Myers had written a song, and he was telling Luckstone about it, and Luckstone said fine, he'd sing it.

"I haven't put it on paper yet—"

"All right, I'll sing it."

"Well, it goes like this—"

"God Almighty, does a man have to know a song to sing it? Get going on your goddam piano, and I'll sing it!"

And he sang it. Nobody but another singer knows how good a singer really is. Sure, I sang his Arlésienne for him. I got a look at his score after Act III, and what he had done was put some words to the slow part, let the baritone sing them, then have baritone and chorus sing them under the fast part, in straight counterpoint. I didn't even bother to look what the words were. I bellowed "Auprès de ma blonde, qu'il fait bon, fait bon," and let it go at that. One place I shot past a repeat. The dancers were all frozen on one foot, ready to do the routine again, and there was I, camped on an E that didn't even belong there. He looked up, and I caught his eye, and hung on to it, and marched all around with it, while he spoke to his men and wigwagged to his ballerina. Then he looked up again, and I cut, and yelled, "Ha, ha, ha." He brought his stick down, the show was together again, and I began flapping the cape at the dancers. In the Toreador Song, on the long "Ah" that leads into the chorus, I broke out the cape and made a couple of passes at the bull. Not too much, you understand. A prop can kill a number. But enough that I got that swirl of crimson and yellow into it. It stopped the show, and he let me repeat the second verse.

Some time during the night I had been given a dressing room, and after the last bow I went there. My clothes were there, piled on the table, and Sabini's trunk. Instead of taking off the make-up first, I started with the costume, so he could get away, if he was still around. I had just stripped down to my underwear when the manager came in, to pay me off. He counted out fifty bucks, in fives. While he was doing it the process server came in. He had a summons to appear in court and a writ to attach costumes. It took all the manager and I could do to convince him I wasn't Alessandro Sabini, but after a few minutes he went. I was scared to death he would see the "A. S." on that trunk, and serve the writ anyhow, but he didn't think of that. The conductor came in and thanked me. 'You gave a fine performance, and I'd like you to know it was a pleasure to have somebody up there that could troupe a little."

"Thanks. I'm sorry about that bobble."

"That's what I'm talking about. When you gave me the chance to pull it out of the soup, that was what I call trouping. Anybody can make a mistake, especially when they're shoved out there the way you were, without even a rehearsal. But when you use your head—well, my hat's off to you, that's all."

"They be pleasant words. Thanks again."

"I don't think they even noticed it. Did they, Morris?"

"Notice it? Christ, they give it a hand."

I sat on the trunk, and we lit up, and they began telling me what the production cost, what the hook-up was, and some more things I wanted to know. Up to then I didn't even know their names. The conductor was Albert Hudson, who you've probably heard of by now, and if you haven't you soon will. The manager was Morris Lahr, who you've never heard of, and never will. He runs a concert series in the winter, and manages a couple of singers, and now and then he puts on an opera. There's one like him in every city, and if you ask me they do more for music than the guys that get their name in the papers.

We were fanning along, me in my underwear with my make-up still on, when the door opens and in pops Stoessel, the agent I had been talking to not a week before. He had a little guy with him, around fifty, and they stood looking at me like I was some ape in a cage, and then Stoessel nodded. "Mr. Ziskin, I believe you're right. He's the type. He's the type you been looking for. And he sings good as Eddy."

"I need a big man, Herman. A real Beery type."

"He's better looking than Beery. And younger. A hell of a sight younger."

"But he's rugged. You know what I mean? Tough. But in the picture, he's got a heart like all outdoors, and that's where the singing comes in. A accent I don't mind, because why? He's got a heart like all outdoors, and a accent helps it."

"I know exactly what you mean, Mr. Ziskin."

"O.K., then, Herman. You handle it. Three fifty while he's learning English, and then after the script is ready and we start to shoot, five. Six weeks' guarantee, at five hundred."

Stoessel turned to Hudson and Lahr. "I guess Mr. Ziskin don't need any introduction around here. He's interested in this man for a picture. Tell him that much, will you? Then we give him the rest of it."

Lahr didn't act like he was any too fond of Mr. Ziskin, or Stoessel either, for that matter. "Why don't you tell him yourself?"

"He speak English?"

"He did a minute ago."

"Sure, I speak English. Shoot."

"Well, say, that makes it easy. O.K., then, you heard what Mr. Ziskin said. Get your make-up off put on your clothes, and we'll go out and talk."

"We can talk right now."

I was afraid to take my make-up off, for fear he would know me. They still thought I was Sabini, I could see that, because there hadn't been any announcement about me, and I was afraid if he placed me there wouldn't be any three fifty or even one fifty. I was down, that day, and he knew it. "All right, then, we'll talk right now. You heard Mr. Ziskin's proposition. What do you say?"

"I say go climb a tree."

"Say, that's no way to talk to Mr. Ziskin."

"What the hell do you think a singer works for? Fun?"

"I know what they work for. I handle singers."

"I don't know whether you handle singers. Maybe you

handle bums. If Mr. Ziskin has got something to say, let him say it. But don't waste my time talking about three hunded and fifty dollars a week. If it was a day, that would be more like it."

"Don't be silly."

"I'm not being silly. I'm booked straight through to the first of the year, and if I'm going to get out of those contracts it's going to cost me dough. If you want to pay dough, talk. If not, just let's stop where we are."

"What's your idea of dough?"

"I've told you. But I've been wanting to break into pictures, and to get the chance, I'll split the difference with you. I'll do a little better than that. A thousand a week, and it's a deal. But that's rock bottom. I can't cut it, and I can't shade it."

We had it hot for a half hour, but I stuck and they came around. I wanted it in writing, so Stoessel took out a notebook and pen and wrote a memo of agreement, about five lines. I got a buck out of my pants and made him a receipt for that, first of all. That bound them. But when we got that far I had to tell my name. I hated to say John Howard Sharp, but I had to. He didn't say anything. He tore out the leaf, waved it in the air, handed it to Ziskin to sign. "John Howard Sharp—sure, I've heard of him. Somebody was telling about him just the other day."

They went, and a boy came in for Sabini's trunk, and Lahr went out and came back with a bottle and glasses. "Guy has broke into pictures, we got to have a drink on that. . . . Where did you say you were booked?"

"With the Santa Fe, mashing down ballast."

"Happy days."

"Happy days."

"Happy days."

The crowd was gone and she was all alone when I ran down the hill, waving the cape at her. She turned her back on me, started to walk to the bus stop. I pulled out the wad of fives Lahr had given me. "Look, look, look!" She wouldn't even turn her head. I took my coat off her, put it on, and dropped the cape over her shoulders. ". . . I wait very long time."

"*Business! I been talking business.*"

"Yes. Smell very nice."

"Sure we had a drink. But listen: get what I'm telling you. I been talking business."

"I wait very long."

I let her get to the bus stop, but I didn't mean to ride on a bus. I began yelling for a taxi. There weren't any, but a car pulled up, a car from a limousine service. "Take you any place you want to go, sir. Rates exactly the same as the taxis—"

Did I care what his rates were? I shoved her in, and that did it. She tried to stay sore, but she felt the cushions, and when I took her in my arms she didn't pull away. There weren't any kisses yet, but the worst was over. I halfway liked it. It was our first row over a little thing. It made me feel she belonged to me.

We went to the Derby and had a real feed. It was the first time I had been in a decent place for a year. But I didn't break the big news until we were back at the hotel, undressing. Then I kind of just slid into it. "Oh, by the way, I got a little surprise for you."

"Surprise?"

"I got a job in pictures."

"Cinema?"

"That's right. A thousand a week."

"Oh."

"Hell, don't you get it? We're rich! A thousand a week —not pesos, dollars! Three thousand, six hundred pesos every week! Why don't you say something?"

"Yes, very nice."

I didn't mean a thing to her! But when I took the cape, and stood up there in my drawers, and sang the Toreador song at her, like I had at the Bowl, that talked. She clapped her hands, and sat on the bed, and I gave her the whole show. The phone rang. The desk calling, to ask me to shut up. I said O.K., but send up a boy. When he came I gave him a five and told him to get us some wine. He was back in a few minutes and we got a little tight, the way we had that night in the church. After a while we went to bed, and a long while after that she lay in my arms, running her fingers through my hair. "You like me?"

"Yes, much."

"Did I sing all right?"

"Very pretty."

"Were you proud of me?"

". . . You very fonny fallow, you, Hoaney. Why I be proud? I no sing."

"But *I* sang."

"Yes. I like. Very much."

8

I DIDN'T LIKE HOLLYWOOD. I didn't like it partly because of the way they treated a singer, and partly because of the way they treated her. To them, singing is just something you buy, for whatever you have to pay, and so is acting, and so is writing, and so is music, and anything else they use. That it might be good for its own sake is something that hasn't occurred to them yet. The only thing they think is good for its own sake is a producer that couldn't tell Brahms from Irving Berlin on a bet, that wouldn't know a singer from a crooner until he heard twenty thousand people yelling for him one night, that can't read a book until the scenario department has had a synopsis made, that can't even speak English, but that is a self-elected expert on music, singing, literature, dialogue, and photography, and generally has a hit because somebody lent him Clark Gable to play in it. I did all right, you understand. After the first tangle with Ziskin I kind of got the hang of how you handle things out there to get along. But I never liked it, not even for a second.

It turned out he wasn't the main guy on his lot, or even a piece of the main guy. He was just one producer there, and when I showed up the next morning he seemed even to have forgot my name. I had his piece of paper, so they had to pay me, but I wandered around for a week not knowing what I was supposed to do or where I was supposed to do it. You see, he didn't have his script ready. But my piece of paper said six weeks, and I meant to collect on it. After four or five days they shoved me in what they call a B picture, a Western about a cowboy that hates sheep and the sheep man's daughter, but then he finds some sheep caught in a blizzard and brings them home safe, and that fixes it all up. I couldn't see where it fixed anything, but it wasn't my grief. They had bought some news-reel stuff on sheep caught in the snow, and that seemed to be the main reason for the picture. The director didn't know I could sing, but I got him to let me spot a couple of campfire songs, and on the blizzard stuff, Git Along, Little Dogies, Git Along.

They finished it toward the end of September, and gave it a sneak preview in Glendale. I thought it was so lousy I went just out of curiosity to see how bad they would razz it. They ate it up. On the snow stuff, every time I came around the bend with a lamb in my arms, breaking trail for the sheep, they'd clap and stamp and whistle. Out in the lobby, after it was over, I caught just a few words between the producer, the director, and one of the writers. "B picture hell—it's a feature!"

"Christ, would that help the schedule! We're three behind now, and if we can make an extra feature out of this, would that be a break! Would that be a break!"

"We got to do retakes."

"We got to do it bigger, but it'll get by."

"It'll cost dough, but it's worth it."

She hadn't come with me. We were living in an apartment on Sunset by that time, and she was going to night school, trying to learn how to read. I went home and she had just gone to bed with her reader, Wisdom of the Ages, a book of quotations from poetry, all in big type, that she practiced on. I got out the guitar and some blank music paper that I had, and I went to work. I split up that song, Git Along, Little Dogies, Git Along, into five-part harmony, one part the straight melody, the other four a quartet obligato in long four-beat and eight-beat notes, and maybe you think it wasn't work. That song is nothing extra to start with, and when you try to plaster polyphonic harmony on top of it, it's a job. But after a while I had it done, and went to bed with her to get a little sleep.

Next morning, before they could get together and really think up something dumb, I got the producer, the director, the writer and the sound man together in the producer's office, and I laid it down to them.

"All right, boys, I heard a little of what you said last night. You thought you had a B picture here, and now you find out if it's fixed up a little bit, you can get away with it for a feature. You want to do retakes, put some more money in it, do it bigger. Now listen to me. You don't have to put one extra dime in this if you do what I tell you, and you can make it a wow. The big hit is the snow stuff. You've got at least ten thousand feet of that that you didn't use. I know because I saw it run off one day in the projection room. The problem is, how to get more of that stuff in, and tie it up so it makes sense so they don't get tired of it before you've really made full use of it. All right, this is what we do. We rip out that sound track where I'm singing, and make another one. I do that song, but after the first verse I come in, singing over top of myself, see? My own voice, singing an obbligato to myself on the verse. Then when that's done, I come in and sing another one on top of that. Then I come in on top of that, so before the end of it, there's five voices there—all me—light falsetto for the tenor part, heavier for the middle point, and plenty of beef in the bass. Then we repeat it. At the repeat, we start a tympanum, a kettle drum, just light at first, but keeping time to the slug of his feet, and when he gets in sight of the ranch-house we bang hell out of it, and let the five-part harmony swell out so the thing really gets there. All during that, you keep cutting in the snowy stuff, but not straight cuts. Slow dissolves, so you get a kind of dream effect, to go with the cock-eyed harmony on that song.

And it doesn't cost you a dime. Nothing but my pay, and you've got me anyhow, for another two weeks. How does it hit you?"

The producer shook his head. His name was Beal, and he and the director and the writer had been listening like it was merely painful, my whole idea. "It's impossible."

"Why is it impossible? You can put all those parts on your loops, I know you can. After you've checked your synchronization, you run them off and make your sound track. It's absolutely possible."

"Listen, we got to do it big, see? That means we got to do retakes, we got to put more production in, and if I got to spend money, I'd a hell of a sight rather spend it on that than on this. This way you say, I got to pay an arranger, I got to hire an orchestra—"

"Arranger, hell. It's already arranged. I've got the parts right here. And what orchestra?"

"For the kettle drum, and—"

"I play the kettle drum myself. On every repeat of the song, I tune it up. Just a little higher, to get a sense of climax, a little louder, a little faster. Don't you get it? They're getting near home. It'll build. It'll give you what you're looking for, it—"

"Nah, it's too tricky. Besides, how can a goddamn cowboy be singing quartets with himself out there in the snow? They wouldn't never believe it. Besides, we got to pump up the rest of the picture, the beginning—"

"O.K., we'll do that, and then they'll believe everything. Look."

It had suddenly popped in my mind about my voice coming back at me, that night in the arroyo, and I knew I had something. "In that campfire song, the second one, Home On The Range, we do a little retake and show him singing it at the mountains. His voice comes back, in an echo. It surprises him. He likes it. He begins to fool around with it, and first thing you know, he's singing a duet with himself, and then maybe a trio. We don't do much with it. Just enough that they like it, and we establish it. Then in the snow scene it's not tricky at all. It's his own voice coming back at him from all over that range—out there all alone, bringing home those sheep.

They can believe it then, can't they? What's tricky now?"

"It's not enough. We got to do retakes."

Up to then the sound man had sat like he was asleep. He sat up now and began to make marks on a piece of paper. "It can be done."

"Even if it can be done, it's no good."

"It can be done, and it's good."

"Oh, you're telling me what's good?"

"Yeah, I'm telling you."

The technical guys on a lot, they're not like the rest of them. They know their stuff, and they don't take much off a producer or anybody. "You went and bought ten thousand feet of the prettiest snow stuff I ever saw, and then what did you do? You threw out all but four hundred feet of it. It's a crime to waste that stuff, and the lousy way you fixed up the story, there's no way to get it in but the way this guy says. All right then, do like he says, and get it in. It'll build, just like he says it will. You'll get all those angle shots in, all those far shots of miles of sheep going down that mountain, all but the little bits that you never even tried to get in before, and then toward the end of it, the ranchhouse where they're getting near home. I'll give him a light mix on the first of it, and on all the far shots, and when we get near the end —we cut her loose. That kettle drum, that's O.K. It'll get that tramp-tramp feel to it, and go with the music. The echoes on Home On The Range I can work with no trouble at all. It's O.K. And it's O.K. all down the line. It's the only chance you got. Because listen: either this is a little epic all by itself, or it's a goddam cheapie not worth hell room. Take your pick."

"Epic! That's what I've been trying to get."

"Well then, this is how you get it."

"All right, then, fix it up like he says. Let me know when you've got something for me to look at."

So he, I, and the cutter went to work. When I say work I mean work. It was sing, rewrite the parts, test the mix, run it off, and do it all over again from morning to night, and from night to almost morning, but after a couple of weeks we had it done and they gave it another preview, downtown this time, with the newspapers notified.

They clapped, cheered, and gave it a rising vote. The Times next morning said "Woolies" was "one of the most vital, honest, and moving things that had come out of Hollywood in a long time," and that "John Howard Sharp, a newcomer with only featured billing, easily stole the picture, and is star material, unless we miss our guess. He can act, he can sing, and he has that certain indefinable, je-ne-sais-quoi something. He's distinctly somebody to watch."

So the next day eight guys showed up to sell me a car, two to sell me annuities, one to get me to sing at a benefit, and one to interview me for a fan magazine. I was a Hollywood celebrity overnight. When I went on the lot in the afternoon I got a call to report to the office of Mr. Gold, president of the company. Ziskin was there, and another producer named London. You'd have thought I was the Duke of Windsor. It seemed I wasn't to wait till Ziskin got his script ready. I was to go into another one that was waiting to shoot. They had been dickering with John Charles Thomas for it, but he was tied up. They thought I would do just as well, because I was younger and bigger and looked the part better. It was about a singing lumberjack that winds up in grand opera.

I said I was glad they liked my work, and everything was fine if we could come to terms on money. They looked kind of funny, and wanted to know what I was talking about. We had our agreement, and I was pretty well paid for a man that started in pictures just a little while ago.

"We did have an agreement, Mr. Gold."

"And we still got it."

"It ran out today."

"Get his contract, Ziskin."

"He's sewed for five years, Mr. Gold, absolutely for five years from the date on the contract, with options every six months, same as all our talent, with a liberal increase, two fifty I think it was, every time we take up our option. A fine, generous contract, and frankly, Mr. Sharp, I am much amazed by the attitude you're taking. That won't get you nowheres in pictures."

"Get his contract."

So they sent down for my contract, and a secretary came up with it, and Gold took a look at it, put his thumb on the amounts and handed it over. "You see?"

"Yeah, I see everything but a signiature."

"This is a file copy."

"Don't try to kid me. I haven't signed any contract. That may be the contract you were going to offer me, but the only thing that's been signed is this thing here, that ran out today."

I fished out the memo I had got off Ziskin that night in the dressing-room. Gold began to roar at Ziskin. Ziskin began to roar at the secretary. "Yes, Mr. Ziskin, the contract came through at least a month ago, but you gave me strict orders not to have any contracts signed until you gave your personal approval, and it's been on your desk all that time. I've called it to your attention."

"I been busy. I been cutting Love Is Love."

The secretary went. Ziskin went. London looked sore. Gold began drumming on his desk with his fingers. "O.K., then. If you want a little more dough, something like that, I guess we can boost you a little. Tell you what we do. We won't bother with any new contract. You can sign this one here, and we'll take up the first option right away, and that'll give you twelve fifty. No use quarreling about a few hundred bucks. Report on the set tomorrow morning to Mr. London here, and you better be going down and getting measured for your costumes so you can start."

"I'm afraid twelve fifty won't do, Mr. Gold."

"Why not?"

"I prefer to work by the picture."

"O.K., then. Let's see, this is on a six-week shooting schedule, that'll make seven and a half for the picture. I'll have new contracts drawn up this afternoon with corresponding options."

"I'm afraid that won't do either."

"What the hell are you getting at?"

"I want fifty thousand for the picture, with no options. I want to work, but I want every picture a separate deal. For this one, fifty thousand. When we see how that goes, we'll talk again."

"Talk like you had good sense."

"Listen, I've been out here a little while now, I know what you pay, and fifty thousand is the price. Very low it is, too, but as you say, I'm new here, and I've got to be reasonable."

London left, talking over his shoulder as he went. "Stop work on the sets. I'll wait for Thomas. If I can't get him I'll take Tibbett, and if I can't get him I'll put an actor in and dub the sound. But I'll be goddamned if I'm paying fifty grand to this punk."

"Well, you heard him, Mr. Sharp. He's the producer. Fifty thousand is out of the question. We might up that seven and and a half to ten, but that would be top. The picture can't stand it, Mr. Sharp. After all, we know what our productions cost."

"I heard him, and now in case you didn't hear me, I'll say it over again. The price is fifty thousand. Now beginning tomorrow I'm taking a little rest. I've been working hard, and I'm tired. But one week from today, if I don't hear from you, I'm taking the plane for New York. I've got plenty of work waiting for me there, and get this: I'm not just talking. I'm going."

"I hate to see you be so foolish."

"Fifty, or I go."

"Why—pictures could make you rich. And you can't get away with this. You're trying to put one over on us. You'll be blackballed all over Hollywood. No studio will have you."

"To hell with that. Fifty or I don't work."

"Oh, to hell with it, hey? I'll goddam well see that you don't work in Hollywood. We'll see if a lousy ham actor can put one like that over on Rex Gold."

"Sit down."

He sat, and he sat pretty quick. "Once more. Fifty or I'm going to New York. You got a week."

"Get out of my office."

"On my way."

I had bought a little car by then, and every day we would start out early for the beach or some place, and every day when we got back, around one o'clock, so she could take her siesta, there would be a memo to call Mr.

98

Ziskin, or Mr. London, or somebody. I never called. Around five o'clock they would call again, and it would turn out that if I would go over and apologize to Mr. Gold, there might be an adjustment on the price, say up to fifteen thousand, or something like that. I did like hell go over and apologize. I said I had done nothing to apologize for, and the price was still fifty thousand. Somewhere around the fifth day they got up to twenty-five. We were at the Burbank airport, going out to the plane, before they came around. A guy ran up, waving signed contracts. I looked them over. They said fifty thousand, but called for three pictures, one each at that price. I thought fast, and said if they'd pay for my tickets it was all right. He snatched them out of my hand before I even finished. Next day I went into Gold's office and said I heard he wanted to apologize. He took that for a gag and we shook hands.

All that time I was making "Woollies," I hardly saw her at all. By the time I got in from the lot, around seven or eight o'clock, she would be gone to night school. I'd eat dinner alone, then go and get her, and we'd have a little snack at the Derby or somewhere. Then it would be time to go home and go to sleep. Believe me, you work on a picture lot, and don't let anybody tell you different. She'd be still asleep when I left in the morning, and the next night it would be the same thing over again. But that week I took off, we did go out and buy her some clothes. We got four or five dresses, and a fur coat, and some more hats. She loved the fur coat. It was mink, and she would stroke it the way she stroked the bull's ears. And she looked swell in it. But the hats she couldn't get the hang of at all. Between me and the saleswoman, we managed to fix her up with a few that seemed to be all right, a kind of soft brown felt hat that would do for regular dresses and that went nice with the coat, and a big filmy one for night, and a little one for knocking around in the morning, or at night school, and two or three that went with what the saleswoman called sports dresses, the kind of thing they wear at the beach. But she never could get it through her head which hat went with which dress.

We'd start out for the beach, and she'd come out of the bedroom with white dress, white shoes, white handbag, and the big floppy evening hat. Or she'd start out in the afternoon with a street dress on, and the fur coat, and one of the sports hats. And I'd have a hard time arguing her out of it, make her put on what she ought to have. "But the hat is very pretty. I like."

"It's pretty, but you can't wear evening hats to the beach. It looks funny. It's all wrong."

"But why?"

"I don't know why. You just can't do it."

"But I like."

"Well, can't you just take my word for it?"

"I no understand."

And then this thing happened that finished me with Hollywood, and everything about Hollywood, for good. Maybe you don't know what it's like to be a big Hollywood actor. Well, it's about like being the winning jockey in the Irish Sweepstakes, only worse. You can't turn around that somebody isn't asking you to some little party he's giving, or begging your autograph for some kid that is home sick in bed, or to take space in some trade paper, or to sing at some banquet for a studio executive. Some of that stuff I had to do, like the banquet, but the parties, I ducked by saying I had to work. But when "Paul Bunyan" was finished, and I was waiting around for re-takes, I got this call from Elsa Chadwick, that played opposite me in it, asking me to a little party at her house the next night, just a few friends, and would I sing? She caught me with my mouth hanging open, and I couldn't think of anything to say. I mumbled something about having an engagement to take a lady to dinner, and she began to gurgle that I should bring her. Of course I should bring her. She would expect us both around nine.

I didn't know what Juana was going to say, but instead of balking, she wanted to go. "Oh yes. I like, very much. This Miss Chadwick, I have seen her, in the cinema. She is very nice."

Next day, early, I was called over to re-shoot a scene, and I forgot about the party till I got home. Juana was under the shower, getting ready to go. By that time I had a Hollywood suit of evening clothes, and I put them on, and went out in the living-room and waited. In about a half hour she came out, and I got this feeling in the pit of my stomach. She had gone out, all by herself, and bought a special dress for the party. Do you know what a Mexican girl's idea of a party dress is? It's white silk, with red flowers all over it, a red rose in her hair, and white shoes with rhinestone buckles. God knows where she found that outfit. It looked like Ramona on Sunday afternoon. I opened my mouth to tell her it was all wrong but took her in my arms and held her to me. You see, it was all for me. She wanted to wear a red rebozo, instead of a hat. It was evening, and didn't call for a hat, so I said all right. But when she put it on, that made it still worse. Those rebozos are hand-woven, but they're cotton, like everything else in Mexico. I'd hate to tell you what she looked like with that dress, and those shoes, and that cotton shawl over her head.

Chadwick went into a gag clinch with me when we came in, but when she saw Juana the grin froze on her face and her eyes looked like a snake's. There were twenty or thirty people there, and she took us in and introduced us, but she didn't take us around. She stood with us, near the door, rattled off the names in a hard voice. Then she sat Juana down, got her a drink, put some cigarettes beside her, and that was all. She didn't go near her again, and neither did any of the other women. I sat down on the other side of the room, and in a minute they were all around me, particularly the women, with a line of Hollywood chatter, all of it loud and most of it off color. They haven't got the Hollywood touch till they cuss like mule-skinners and peddle the latest dirty crack that was made on some lot. I fed it back like they gave it, but I was watching Juana. I thought of the soft way she talked, and how she never had said a dirty word in her life, and the dignified way she had stood there while she was being introduced, and the screechy way they had acted. And I felt something getting thick in my throat. Who were they to leave her there all alone with a drink and a pack of Camels?

George Schultz, that had done the orchestrations for

"Bunyan," went over to the piano and started to play. "Feel like singing, boy?"

"Just crazy to sing."

"Little Traviata?"

"Sure."

"O.K., give."

He went into the introduction of *Di Provenza il Mar.* But this thing in my throat was choking me. I went over to Juana. "Come on. We're going home."

"You no sing?"

"No. Come on."

"Hey, where are you? That's your cue."

"Yeah?"

"You're supposed to come in."

"I'm not coming in."

"What the hell is this?"

We went out and put on our things and Chadwick followed us to the door. "Well, you don't seem to enjoy my little party?"

"Not much."

"It's mutual. And the next time you come don't show up with a cheap Mexican tart that—"

That's the only time a woman ever took a cuff in the puss from John Howard Sharp. She screamed and three or four guys came out there, screen he-men, all hot to defend the little woman and show how tough they were. I stepped back to let them out. I wanted them out. I was praying they'd come out. They didn't. I took Juana by the arm and started for the car. "There won't be any next time, baby."

"They no like me, Hoaney?"

"They didn't act like it."

"But why?"

"I don't know why."

"I do something wrong?"

"Not a thing. You were the sweetest one there."

"I no understand."

"You needn't even bother to try to understand. But if they ever pull something like that on you, just let me know. That's all I've got to say. Just let me know."

We went to the Golondrina. It's a Mexican restaurant on Olvera Street, a kind of Little Mexico they've got in Los Angeles, with mariachis, pottery, jumping beans, bum silverware, and all the rest of it. If she had dressed for me, I was bound she was going to have a good time if I had to stand the whole city on its ear to give it to her. She had it. She had never been there before, but as soon as they spotted her they all came around, and talked, and laughed, and she was back home. The couple in the floor show made up a special verse of their song for her, and she took the flower out of her hair and threw it out there, and they did a dance with it, and gave her some comedy. Their comedy is a lot of bum cucaracha gags, with a lot of belly-scratching and eye-rolling and finger-snapping, but it was funny to her, so it was funny to me. It was the first time I had ever had a friendly feeling toward Mexico.

Then I sang. A big movie shot is an event in that place, but a Mexican would never pull anything, or let you know he was looking at you. I had to call for the guitar myself, but then I got a big hand. I sang to her, and to the girl in the floor show, and whanged out a number they danced to, and then we all sang the Golondrina. It was two o'clock before we left there. When we went to bed I held her in my arms, and long after she was asleep this fury would come over me, about how they had treated her. I knew then I hated Hollywood, and only waited for the day I could clear out of there for good.

Under their contract, they had three months to call me for the next picture, and the way the time was counted, that meant any date up to April 1. It was just before Christmas that I got the wire from the New York agent that she had a tip the Met was interested in me, and would I please, please, let her go ahead on the deal? I began to rave like a crazy man. "Hoaney, why you talk so?"

"Read it! You've been going to school, there's something for you to practice on. Read it, and see what you've been missing all this time."

"What is 'Met'?"

"Just the best opera company in the world, that's all. The big one in New York, and they want me. They want me!—she'd never be sending that unless she knew something. A chance to get back to my trade at last, and here I am sewed up on a lousy contract to make two more pictures that I hate, that aren't worth making, that—"

"Why you make these pictures?"

"I'm under contract, I tell you. I've got to."

"But why?"

I tried to explain contract to her. It couldn't be done. An Indian has never heard of a contract. They didn't have them under Montezuma, and never bothered with them since. "The picture company, you make money for her, yes?"

"Plenty. I don't owe her a dime."

"Then it is right, you go?"

"Right? Did they ever give me anything I didn't take off them with a blackjack? Would they even give me a cup of coffee if I didn't pack them in at the box office? Would they even respect my trade? This isn't about right. It's about some ink on a dotted line."

"Then why you stay? Why you no sing at these Met?"

That was all. If it wasn't right, then to hell with it. A contract was just something that you probably couldn't read anyway. I looked at her, where she was lying on the bed with nothing on but a rebozo around her middle, and knew I was looking across ten thousand years, but it popped in my mind that maybe they weren't as dumb ten thousand years ago as I had always thought. Well, why not? I thought of Malinche, and how she put Cortés on top of the world, and how his star went out like a light when he thought he didn't need her any more. ". . . That's an idea."

"I think you sing at these Met."

"Not so loud."

"Yes."

"I think you're a pretty bright girl."

Next day I hopped over to the Taft Building and saw a lawyer. He begged me not to do anything foolish. "In the first place, if you run out on this contract, they can make your life so miserable that you hardly dare go out of doors without some rat shoving a summons at you with a dollar bill in it, and you'll have to appear in court. Do you know what that means? Do you know what those blue summonses did to Jack Dempsey? They cost him a title, that's all. They can sue you. They can sew you up with injunctions. They can just make you wish you never even heard of the law, or anything like it."

"That's what we got lawyers for, isn't it?"

"That's right. You can get a lawyer there in New York, and he can handle some of it. And he'll charge you plenty. But you can't hire as many lawyers as they've got."

"Listen, can they win, that's all I want to know. Can they bring me back? Can they keep me from working?"

"Maybe they can't. Who knows? But—"

"That's all I want to know. If I've got any kind of a fighting chance, I'm off."

"Not so fast. Maybe they don't even try. Maybe they think it's bad policy. But this is the main point: You run out on this contract, and your name is mud in Hollywood from now on—"

"I don't care about that."

"Oh yes you do. How do you know how well you do in grand opera?"

"I've been in it before."

"And out of it before, from all I hear."

"My voice cracked up."

"It may again. This is my point. The way Gold is building you up, Hollywood is sure for you, as sure as anything can be, for quite some time to come. It makes no difference to him if your voice cracks up. He'll buy a voice. He'll dub your sound for you—"

"Not for me he won't."

"Will you for Christ sake stop talking about art? I'm talking about money. I'm telling you that if your pictures really go, he'll do anything. He'll play you straight. He'll fix it up anyway that makes you look good. And most of all, he'll pay you! More than any opera company will ever pay you! It's a backlog for you to fall back on, *but*—"

"Yeah, but?"

"Only as long as you play ball. Once you start some funny business, not only he, but every other picture man in Hollywood turns thumbs down, and that's the end of you, in pictures. There's no black-list. Nobody calls anybody up. They just hear about it, and that's all. I can give you names, if you want them, of bright boys like you that thought they could jump a Hollywood contract, and tell you what happened to them. These picture guys hate each other, they cut each other's throats all the time, but when something like this happens, they act with a unanimity that's touching. Now, have you seen Gold?"

"I thought I'd see you first."

"That's all right. Then there's no harm done. Now before you do anything rash, I want you to see him. There may be no trouble at all. He may want you to sing at the Met, just for build-up. He may be back of it, for all you know. Get over and see him, see if you can fix it up. After lunch, come back and see me."

So I went over and saw Gold. He wanted to talk about the four goals he made in the polo game the day before. When we did get around to it he shook his head. "Jack, I know what's good for you, even if you don't. I read the signs all the time, it's my business to know, and they'll all tell you Rex Gold don't make many mistakes. Jack, grand opera's through."

"What?"

"It's through, finished. Sure, I dropped in at the Metropolitan when I was east last week, saw Tosca, the same opera that we do a piece of in Bunyan, and I'd hate to tell you what they soaked me for the rights on it, too. And what do I see? Well, boy, I'm telling you, we just made a bum out of them. That sequence in our picture is so much better than their job, note for note, production for production, that comparison is just ridiculous. Grand opera is through. Because why? Pictures have stepped in and done it so much better than they can do it that they can't get by any more, that's all. Opera is going the same way the theatre is going. Pictures have just rubbed them out."

"Well—before it dies, I'd like to have a final season in

106

it. And I don't think the Metropolitan stamp would hurt me any, even in pictures."

"It would ruin you."

"How?"

"I've been telling you. Grand opera is through. Grand opera pictures are through. The public is sick of them. Because why? Because they got no more material. They've done Puccini over and over again, they've done La Bohème and Madame Butterfly so much we even had to fall back on La Tosca for you in Bunyan, and after you've done your Puccini, what you got left? Nothing. It's through, washed up. We just can't get the material."

"Well—there are a couple of other composers."

"Yeah, but who wants to listen to them?"

"Almost anybody, except a bunch of Kansas City yaps that think Puccini is classical, as they call it."

"Oh, so you don't like Puccini?"

"Not much."

"Listen, you want to find out who's the best painter in the world, what do you do? You try to buy one of his pictures. Then you find out what you got to pay. O.K., you want to find out who's the best composer in the world, you try to buy some of his music. Do you know what they charged me, just for license rights, on that scene you did from Tosca? You want to know? Wait, I'll get the canceled vouchers. I'll show you. You wouldn't believe it."

"Listen, Puccini has been the main asset of that publishing house for years, and everybody in grand opera knows it, and that's got nothing to do with how good he is. It's because he came in after we began to get copyright laws, and because he was handled from the beginning for every dime that could be got out of him from guys like you. If you're just finding that out, it may prove you don't know anything about opera, but it doesn't prove anything about Puccini."

"Why do you suppose guys like me pay for him?"

"Probably because you knew so little about opera you couldn't think of anything else. If you had let me help on that script, I'd have fixed you up with numbers that wouldn't have cost you a dime."

"A swell time to be saying that."

"To hell with it. You got Tosca, and it's all right. I'm talking about a release for the rest of the season to go on at the Met."

"And I'm talking about what's good for one of our stars. There's no use our arguing about composers, Jack. Maybe you know what's pretty but I know what sells. And I tell you grand opera is through. And I tell you that from now on you lay off it. The way I'm building you up, we're going to take that voice of yours, and what are we going to do with it? Use it on popular stuff. The stuff you sing better than anybody else in the business. The stuff that people want to hear. Lumberjack songs, cowboy songs, mountain music, jazz—you can't beat it! It's what they want! Not any of this tra-la-la-la-la-la! Christ, that's an ear-ache! It's a back number. Look, Jack: From now on, you forget you ever were in grand opera. You give it to them down-to-earth! Right down there where they want it! You get me, Jack? You get me?"

"I get you."

"What did Gold say?"

"He said no."

"I had an idea that was how he felt. I had him on the phone just now, about something else, and I led around to you in a way that didn't tip it you had been in, but he was telling the world where he stood. Well, I'd play along with him. It's tough, but you can't buck him."

"If I do, what did you say my name would be?"

"Mud. M-U-D, mud."

"In Hollywood?"

"Yes, in Hollywood."

"That's all I wanted to know. What do I owe you?"

When I got home there were four more telegrams, saying the thing was hot, if I wanted it, and a memo New York had been calling. I looked at my watch. It was three o'clock. I called the airport. They had two seats on the four-thirty plane. She came in. "Well, Juana, there they are, read them. The abogado says no, a hundred times no. What do I do?"

"You sing Carmen at these Met?"

"I don't know. Probably."

"Yes, I like."

"O.K., then. Get packed."

9

I MADE MY DEBUT in Lucia right after New Year's, sang standard repertoire for a month, began to work in. It felt good to be back with the wops. Then I got my real chance when they popped me on three days' notice into Don Giovanni. I had a hell of a time getting them to let me do the serenade my way, with a real guitar, and play it myself, without the orchestra. The score calls for a prop mandolin, and that's the way the music is written, but I hate all prop instruments on the stage, and hate to play any scene where I have to use one. There's no way you can do it that it doesn't look phoney. I made a gain when I told them that the guitar was tradition, that Garcia used to do it that way, but I lost all that ground when somebody in the Taste Department decided that a real guitar would look too much like the Roxy, and for a day it was all off again. Then I got Wurlitzer's to help me out. They sent down an instrument that was a beauty. It was dark, dull spruce, without any pearl, nickel, or highlights on it of any kind, and it had a tone you could eat with a spoon. When I sounded off on that, that settled it.

I wanted to put it up a half tone, so I could get it in the key of three flats, but I didn't. It's in the key of two sharps, the worst key there is for a singer, especially the high F sharp at the end, that catches a baritone all wrong, and makes him sound coarse and ropy. The F sharp is not in the score, but it's tradition and you have to sing it. God knows why Mozart ever put it in that key, unless it's because two sharps is the best key there is for a mandolin, and he let his singer take the rap so he could bring the accompaniment to life.

But I tuned with the orchestra before the act started, and did it strictly in the original key. I made two moves while I was singing it. Between verses I took one step nearer the balcony. At the end, I turned my back on the audience, stepped under the balcony and played the finish, not to them, but to her. On the F sharp, instead of covering up and getting it over quick, I did a *messa di voce*, probably the toughest order a singer ever tries to deliver. You start it p, swell to ff, pull back to p again, and come off it. My tone wasn't round, but it was pure, and I got away with it all right. They broke into a roar, the bravos yipped out all over the house, and that was the beginning of this stuff that you read, that I was the greatest since Bispham, the peer of Scotti, and all the rest of it. Well, I was the peer of Scotti, or hope I was. They've forgotten by now how bad Scotti really was. He could sing, and he was the greatest actor I ever saw, but his voice was just merely painful. What they paid no attention to at all, mentioned like it was nothing but a little added feature, was the guitar. You can talk about your fiddle, your piano, and your orchestra, and I've got nothing to say against them. But a guitar has moonlight in it.

Don Giovanni, the Marriage of Figaro, Thaïs, Rigoletto, Carmen, and Traviata, going bigger all the time, getting toward the middle of February, and still nothing from Gold. No notification to report, no phone calls, nothing. It was Ziskin's picture I was supposed to do next. I saw by the papers he was in town and that night saw him in Lindy's, but I saw him first and we ducked out and went somewhere else. He looked just as foolish as ever, and I began to tell myself he still didn't have his script ready, and I might win by default.

The Hudson-to-Horn hook-up was something the radio people had been working on for a year, and God knows how many ministers, ambassadors, and contact men had to give them a hand, because most of those stations south of the Rio Grande are government-owned, and so are the Canadian. Then after they put it over, they had a hard job selling the time, because they were asking plenty for it, and every country had to get its cut. Finally they peddled it to Panamier. The car was being put out mainly for export, and the hook-up gave it what it needed. The next thing was: Who were they going to feature on the hour, now they had sold it? They had eight names on their list, the biggest in the business, starting with Grace Moore and ending with me. I moved up a couple of notches when I told them I could do spig songs in Spanish. I couldn't, but I figured I was in bed with the right person to learn. Then Paul Bunyan opened, and I went up to the top. I can't tell you what the picture had. Understand, for my money no picture is any good, really any good, but this one was gay and made you feel you wanted to see it over again. The story didn't make any sense at all, but maybe it was because it was so cock-eyed you got to laughing. One place in there they cut in the Macy parade, the one they hold about a month before Christmas, with a lot of balloons coming down Broadway in the shape of animals. One of the balloons was a cow, and when they cut them loose, with prizes offered to whoever finds them, this one floats clear out over Saskatchewan and comes down on the trees near the lumber camp. Then the lumberjack that I was supposed to be, the one that has told them all he's really Paul Bunyan, says it's Babe, the Big Blue Ox that's come down from heaven to pay him a Christmas visit. Then he climbs up in a tree and sings to it, and the lumberjacks sing to it, and believe it or not, it did things to you. Then when the sun comes up and they see what gender Babe really is, they go up the tree after the guy to lynch him, but somebody accidentally touches a cigar to the cow and she blows up with such a roar that all the trees they were supposed to cut down are lying flat on the ground, and they decide it was Mrs. Babe.

That clinched me for the broadcast, and they ate it up when I told them how to put the show together so it would sell cars. "We open up with the biggest, loudest, five-tone, multiple-action horn you can find, and if you think that's not important, I tell you I've been down there, and I know what you've got to give them to sell cars. You've got to have a horn; first, last, and all the time you've got to have a horn. I take pitch from that and go into the *Golondrina*, for the spig trade, blended in with My Pal Babe, for the Canadian trade. I'll write that little medley myself, and that's our signature. Then we repeat it, you put your announcer in, and after he stops we go right on. We do light Mexican numbers, then we'll turn right around and do some little French-Canadian numbers, then one light American number, when it's time for the announcer again. Then we do a grand opera number and so on for as much time as we've got, and any comedy you want to put in, that's O.K., too, but watch they can understand it. On your car, plug the horn, the lock on the gas tank, the paint job, the speed and the low gas consumption. That's all. Leave out about the brakes, the knee-action, and all that. They never heard of it, and you're just wasting your time. Better let me write those plugs, and you let your announcers translate them. And first, last, and again: Sound that horn."

They stuck together a program the way I said, and we made a record of it one morning with the studio orchestra, then went in an audition room and ran it off. It sounded like something. The advertising man liked it, and the Panamier man was tickled to death with it. "It's got speed to it, you know what I mean? 'Gangway for the Panamier Eight, she's coming down the road!'—that's what it says. And the theme song is a honey. Catches them north, south, and in the middle. Boys, we got something now. That's set. No more if, as, and but about it." I began to feel good. Why did I want that broadcast? Because it would pay me four thousand a week. Because they treated me good. Because I had had that flop, and I could get back at Mexico. Because it made me laugh. Because I could say hello to Captain Conners, wherever he was out there, listening to it. In other words, for no reason. I just wanted it.

That was around the first of March, and they would go

on the air in three weeks, as soon as they could place ads in the newspapers all up and down the line, and get more cars freighted out, to make deliveries. By that time I had kidded myself that Ziskin would never have his script ready, and that I could forget about Hollywood the rest of my life. I woke up after I left them that day, and walked down to the opera house for the matinee Lucia. A messenger was there, with a registered letter from Gold, telling me to report March 10. I was a little off that day, and missed a cue.

What I did about it was nothing at all, except get the address of a lawyer in Radio City that made a specialty of big theatrical cases. Three days later I got a wire from the Screen Actors' Guild, telling me that as I had made no acknowledgment of Gold's notification to report, the case had been referred to them, that I was bound by a valid contract, and that unless I took steps to comply with it at once, they would be compelled to act under their by-laws, and their agreement with the producers. I paid no attention to that either.

Next morning while I was having a piano run-through of the Traviata duet with a new soprano they were bringing out, a secretary came up to the rehearsal room and told me to please go at once to a suite in the Empire State Building, that it was important. I asked the soprano if she minded doing the rest of it after lunch. When I got up to the Empire State Building, I was brought into a big office paneled in redwood, and marked "Mr. Luther, private." Mr. Luther was an old man with a gray cutaway suit, a cheek as pink as a young girl's, and an eye like blue agate. He got up, shook hands, told me how much he had enjoyed my singing, said my Marcello reminded him of Sammarco, and then got down to business. "Mr. Sharp, we have a communication here from a certain Mr. Gold, Rex Gold, informing us that he has a contract with you, and that any further employment of you on our part, after March 10, will be followed by legal action on his part. I don't know what legal action he has in mind, but

I thought it would be well if you came in and, if you can, inform me what he means, if you know."

"You're the attorney for the opera house?"

"Not regularly, of course. But sometimes when somebody is in Europe, they refer things to me."

"Well—I have a contract with Gold."

"For motion pictures, I judge?"

"Yes."

I told him about it, and made it pretty plain I was through with pictures, contract or no contract. He listened and smiled, and seemed to get it all, why I wanted to sing in opera and all the rest of it. "Yes, I can understand that. I understand it very well. And of course, considering the success we're having with you here, I should certainly hesitate to take any step, or give any advice, that would lose you to us at the height of the season. Of course, a telegram unsupported by any other documents is hardly ground for us to make a decision, and in fact we are not bound to take cognizance of contracts made by our singers until a court passes on them, or in some way compels us to. Just the same—"

"Yes?"

"Have you had any communication from Mr. Gold, aside from his letter of notification?"

"Nothing at all. I did have a wire from the Screen Actors' Guild. But that's all."

"The—what was that again?"

I had the wire in my pocket, and showed it to him. He got up and began to walk around the office. "Ah— you're a member of this Guild?"

"Well—everybody is that works in pictures."

"It's an affiliate of Equity, isn't it?"

"I'm not sure. I think so."

". . . I don't know what their procedure is. It's recently organized, and I haven't heard much about it. But I confess, Mr. Sharp, this makes things very awkward. Contracts, court cases—these things I don't mind. After all, that's what I'm here for, isn't it? But I should be very loath to give any advice that would get the company into any mess with the Federation of Musicians. You realize what's involved here, don't you?"

"No, I don't."

"As I say, I don't know the procedure of your Screen Actors' Guild, but if they took the matter up with the musicians, and we had some kind of mess on our hands, over your singing here until you had adjudicated your troubles with your own union—Mr. Sharp, I simply have a horror of it. The musicians are one of the most intelligent, co-operative, and sensible unions we have, and yet, any dispute, coming at the height of the season—!"

"Meaning what?"

"I don't know. I want to think about it."

I went out, had a sandwich and some coffee, and went back to the rehearsal hall. We just about got started when the same secretary came up and said the radio people wanted me to come up right away, that it was terribly important, and would I please make it as soon as I could. The soprano went into an act that blistered the varnish off the piano. At plain and fancy cussing, the coloraturas, I think, are the best in the business. I got out on the street, tried to figure out which was uptown and which down. I thought about Jack Dempsey.

They were all up there, the advertising man, the Panamier man, the broadcasting men, all of them, and there was hell to pay. They had had a wire from Gold, forbidding them to use My Pal Babe, or any part of it, else be sued up to the hilt, and warning them not to use me. The Panamier man raved like an animal. I listened and began to get sore. "What the hell is he talking about? You can use that song. I don't know much about law, but I know that much—"

"We can't use it! We can't use a note of it! It's his! And those ads have gone out to two hundred key newspapers. We got to kill them by wire, we got to get up a whole new program—Christ, why didn't you tell us about this thing? Why did you let us start all this knowing you had that contact?"

"Will you just hold your horses till tonight?"

"For what? Will you tell me that, for what?"

"Till I can see a lawyer?"

"Don't you suppose I've seen a lawyer? Don't you suppose I've had Gold on the phone three times today while I was trying to find where the hell you were? And I've advertised it! I've advertised the goddam theme song! Golondrina, My Babe—don't that sound sick? And I've advertised you—John Howard Sharp, El Panamier Trovador —don't that sound sicker! Get out, for Christ sake—"

"Well you wait? Just till tonight?"

"Yeah, I'll wait. Why not?"

The lawyer was five floors down in the same building. He didn't have redwood paneling in his office. It was just an office, and he was a brisk little guy named Sholto. I laid it out for him. He leaned back, took a couple of calls, and started to talk. 'Sharp, you haven't got a leg to stand on. You made a contract, a contract that any jury would regard as perfectly fair, and the only thing you can do is go through with it. It may reflect credit on your aesthetic conscience that you prefer opera to pictures, but it doesn't reflect any credit on your moral conscience that you jump a contract just because you want to. As well as I can make out this picture company took you when you were a bum, put you on your feet, and now you want to hand them a cross. I don't say you couldn't lick them in court. Nobody can say what a jury is going to do. But you'll be a bum before you ever get to court. Show business is all one gigantic hook-up, Gold knows it frontwards, backwards, crosswise, and on the bias, and you haven't got a chance. You're sewed. You've got to go back and make that picture."

"Just give up everything, now it's breaking for me, go back and make a picture just because that cluck has an idea that opera is through?"

"What the hell are you trying to tell me? One more picture like this Bunyan and you can walk into any opera house in the world, and the place is yours. You're being built into a gallery draw that not one singer in a million can bring into the theatre with him. Haven't you got any brains? These musicals are quota pictures. They go all over the world. They make you famous from Peru to China and from Norway to Capetown, and from Panama to Suez and back again. Don't you suppose opera houses know that? Don't you think the Metropolitan knows it? Do you suppose all this commotion you've caused is just a tribute to your A flat in Pagliacci? It is like hell."

"I haven't sung Pagliacci."

"All right then, Trovatore."

"And that's all you've got to tell me?"

"Isn't it enough?"

I felt so sick I didn't even bother to go up to the broadcasting offices again. I went down, caught a cab, and went home. It was starting to snow. We had sublet a furnished apartment in a big apartment house on East Twenty-second Street, near Gramercy Park. She had liked it because there were Indian rugs around that looked a little like Mexico, and we had been happier there, for six weeks, than I had ever been in my life. She was in bed with a cold. She never could get it through her head what New York weather was like. I sat down and broke the news.

"Well, it's all off. We go back to Hollywood."

"No, please. I like New York."

"Money, Juana. And everything. Back we go."

"But why? We have much money."

"And no place to sing. By tomorrow not even a night club will hire me. Unions. Injunctions. Contracts."

"No, we stay in New York. You take guitar, be a mariachi, just you, Hoaney. You sing for me."

"We got to go back."

I sat beside her, and she kept running her fingers through my hair. We didn't say anything for a long time. The phone rang. She motioned to let it alone. If I hadn't picked it up, our whole life would have been different.

10

WINSTON HAWES, the papers said, was one of the outstanding musicians of his time, the conductor that could really read a score, the man that had done more for modern music than anybody since Muck. He was all of that, but don't get the idea he was ever one of the boys. There was something wrong about the way he thought about music, something unhealthy, like the crowds you always saw at his concerts, and what it was I can only half tell you. In the first place I don't know enough about the kind of people he came from, and in the second place I don't know enough about music. He was rich, and there's something about rich people that's different from the rest of us. They come into the world with an inflated idea of their relation to it, and everything they find in it. I got a little flash into that side of him once, in Paris, when I strolled into an art store to look at some pictures that caught my eye. A guy came in, an American, and began a palaver about prices. And the way that guy talked gave me a whole new slant at his kind. He didn't care about art, the way you do or I do, as something to look at and feel. He wanted to own it. Winston was that way about music. He made a whore out of it. You went to his concerts, but you didn't sit out there at his rehearsals, and see him hold men for an hour overtime, at full pay, just because there was some French horn passage that he liked, and wanted it played over and over again—not to rehearse it, but because of what it did to him. And you didn't walk out with him afterwards, and see him all atremble, and hear him tell how he felt after playing it. He was like some woman that goes to concerts because they give her the right vibrations, or make her feel better, or have some other effect on her nitwit insides. All right, you may think it's cock-eyed to compare him with somebody like that, but I'm telling you that in spite of all his technical skill, he was a hell of a sight nearer to that fat poop than he ever was to Muck. That woman was in him, poodle dog, diamonds, limousine, conceit, cruelty and all, and don't let his public reputation fool you. She has a public reputation too, if she hands out enough money. The day the story broke, they compared him with Stanford White, but I'm telling you that to put Winston Hawes in the same class with Stanford White was a desecration.

You can't own music, the way you can own a picture, but you can own a big hunk of it. You can own a composer, that you put on a subsidy while he's writing a piece for you. You can own an audience that has to come to you to hear that piece if it's going to hear it at all. You can own the orchestra that plays it, and you can own the singer that sings it. I first met him in Paris. I hadn't known him in Chicago. He came from a packing family so rich I never even got within a mile of where they lived. And I didn't look him up, even in Paris. He showed up at my apartment one day, sat down at the piano, played off a couple of songs that were there, and said they were lousy, which they were. Then he got up and asked me how I'd like to sing with his band. I was pretty excited. He had started his Petite Orchestra about a year before, and I had gone to plenty of the concerts, and don't you think they weren't good. He started with thirty men, but by now he was up to forty. He raided everywhere, from the opera orchestras, from the chamber music outfits, and he took anybody he wanted, because he paid about twice what any other band paid. He footed the deficit himself, and he didn't have a man that couldn't have played quartets with Heifetz. What they could do to music, especially modern music, was just make it sound about twice as good as even the composer thought it was. He had some stuff with him he wanted me to do, all of it in manuscript. Part of it was old Italian songs he had dug up, where I would have to do baritone coloratura that had been out of date for a hundred years, and how he knew I could do it I don't know. Part of it was a suite by his first viola, that had never been performed yet. It was tough stuff, music that wouldn't come to life at all without the most exact tone shading. But he gave me six rehearsals—count them, six, something you couldn't believe. Cost didn't mean anything to him. When we went on with it I was with those woodwinds like I was one of the bassoons, and the response was terrific. I took out Picquot, the viola, before I took a call myself, and the whole thing was like something you read about.

That part of it, I wouldn't be telling the truth if I didn't admit it was an adventure in music I'll never forget. I sang for him four times, and each time it was something new, something fresh, and a performance better than you even knew you could give. He had a live stick all right. From some of them you get a beat as dead as an undertaker's handshake, but not from him. He threw it on you like a hypnotist, and you began to roll it out, and yet it was all under perfect control. That's the word to remember, perfect. Perfection is something no singer ever got yet, but under him you came as near to it as you're ever going to get.

That was the beginning of it, and it was quite a while before it dawned on me what he really wanted. As to what he wanted, and what he got, you'll find out soon enough, and I'm not going to tell any more than I have to. But I'd like to make this much clear now: that wasn't what I wanted. What I meant to him and what he meant to me were two different things, but once again, I wouldn't be telling the truth if I didn't admit that what he meant to me was plenty. He took to dropping into my dressing room at the Comique while I was washing up, and he'd tell me some little thing I had done, something he had liked, or sometimes, something he hadn't liked. If he had been giving a concert, maybe he had heard only part of the last act, but there would always be something. You think that didn't mean anything to me? Singing is a funny job. You go out there and take those calls, and it's so exciting that when you get back to your dressing room you want to sing, to cut it loose till the windows rattle, just to let off the steam that excitement makes. You go back there and you'll hear them, especially the tenors, so you'd think they had gone crazy. But that excitement is all from out front, from a mob you only half see and never know, and you get so you'd give anything for somebody, for just one guy, that knew what you were trying to do, that spotted your idea without your telling him, that could appreciate you with his head and not with the palms of his hands. And mind you, it couldn't be just anybody. It has to be somebody you respect, somebody that knows.

I began to wait for that visit. Then pretty soon I was singing to him and to nobody else. We'd walk out, go to a café while I ate, then drop over to his apartment off the Place Vendóme, and have a post-mortem on my performance. Then, little by little, he began making suggestions. Then I began dropping in on him in the morning, and he'd take me through some things I had been doing wrong. He was the best coach in the world, bar none. Then he began to take my acting apart, and put it together again. It was he that cured me of all those operatic gestures I got in Italy. He showed me that good operatic acting consists in as few motions as possible, every one of them calculated for an effect, and every one made to count. He told me about Scotti and how he used to sing the Pagliacci Prologue before he got so bad they couldn't use him in Pagliacci. He made one gesture. At the end of the andante, he held out his hand, and then turned it over, palm up. That was all. It said it. He made me learn a whole new set of gestures, done naturally, and he made me practice for hours singing *sotto voce* without using any gestures at all. That's a tough order, just to stand up there, on a cold stage, and shoot it. But I got so I could do it. And I got so I could take my time, give it to them when I was ready, not before. I began to do better in comedy roles, like Sharpless and Marcello. Taking out all that gingerbread, I could watch timing, and get laughs I never got before. I got so I was with him morning, noon and night, and depended on him like a hophead depends on dope.

Then came my crack-up, and when my money was all gone I had to leave Paris. He stormed about that, wanted to support me, showed me his books to prove that an allowance for me wouldn't even make a dent in his income. But it was that storming that showed me where things had got between him and me, and that I had to break away from him. I went to New York. I tried to find something to do, but there was nothing I could do except sing, and I couldn't sing. That was when this agent kidded me that no matter what shape I was in I was good enough for Mexico, and I went down there.

I had read in some paper that he had disbanded his orchestra in Paris, but I didn't know he was starting his Little Orchestra in New York until I got there. It made me nervous. I dropped in, alone, at his first concert, just so I could say I had, in case I ran into him somewhere. It was the same mob he had had in Paris, clothes more expensive than you would see even at a Hollywood opening, gray-haired women with straight haircuts and men's dinner jackets, young girls looking each other straight in the eye and not caring what you thought, boys following men around, loud, feverish talk out in the foyer, everybody coming out in the open with something they wouldn't dare show anywhere else. His first number was something for strings by Lalo I had heard him play before, and I left right after it. Next day, when I saw the review in the paper I turned the page quick. I didn't want to read it. I had a note from him after Don Giovanni, and shot it right back, and one word written on it, "Thanks," with my initials. I didn't want to write on my own stationery, or he'd know where I was living. I felt funny about asking for opera house stationery. I was afraid not to answer, for fear he'd be around to know why.

So that's how things stood when I was sitting beside Juana and the phone rang. She motioned to let it ring, and I did for a while, but I still hadn't called Panamier, and I knew I had them to talk to, even if I had nothing to say. I answered. But it wasn't Panamier. It was Winston. "Jack! You old scalawag! Where have you been hiding?"

"Why—I've been busy."

"So have I, so busy I'm ashamed of it. I hate to be busy. I like time for my friends. But the moment I'm free as a bird, I've got a fine fire burning, and you can hop in a cab, wherever you are—all I've got is your phone number, and I had a frightful time even getting that—and come up here. I just can't wait to see you."

"Well—that sounds swell, but I've got to go back to Hollywood, right away, probably tomorrow, and that means I'll be tied up every minute, trying to get out of town. I don't see how I could fit it in."

"What did you say? *Hollywood!*"

"Yeah, Hollywood."

"Jack, you're kidding."

"No, I'm a picture star now."

"I know you are. I saw your pictures, both of them. But you can't go back to Hollywood now. Why, you're singing for me, one month from today. I've arranged your whole program. It's out of the question."

"No, I'll have to go."

"Jack, you don't sound like yourself. Don't tell me you've got so big you can't spare one night for a poor dilettante and his band—"

"For Christ sake, don't be silly."

"That sounds more like you. Now what is it?"

"Nothing but what I've told you. I've got to go back there. I don't want to. I hate to. I've tried to get out of it every way I knew, but I'm sewed and I've got no choice."

"That sounds still more like you. In other words, you're in trouble."

"That's it."

"Into the cab and up here. Tell it to Papa."

"No, I'm sorry. I can't. . . . Wait a minute."

She was grabbing for the receiver. I put my hand over it. "Yes, you go."

"I don't want to go."

"You go."

"He's just a guy—I don't want to see."

123

"You go, you feel better, Juana's nose, very snoddy."

"I'll wipe it, then it won't be snoddy."

"Hoaney, you go. Many people call today, all day long. You no here, you no have to talk, no feel bad. Now, you go. I say you gone out. I don't know where. You go, then tonight we talk, you and I. We figure out."

". . . All right, where are you? I'll be up."

He was at a hotel off Central Park, on the twenty-second floor of the tower. The desk told me to go up. I did, found his suite, rang the bell and got no answer. The door was open and I walked in. There was a big living room, with windows on two sides, so you could see all the way downtown and out over the East River, a grand piano at one end, a big phonograph across from that, scores stacked everywhere, and a big fire burning under a mantlepiece. I opened the door that led into the rest of the suite and called, but there wasn't any answer. And then in a second there he was, bouncing in from the hall, in the rough coat, flannel shirt, and battered trousers that he always wore. If you had met him in Central Park you would have given him a dime. "Jack! How are you! I went down to meet you, and they told me you had just gone up! Give me that coat! Give me a smile, for God's sake! That Mexican sunburn makes you look like Othello!"

"Oh, you knew I was in Mexico?"

"Know it! I went down there to bring you back, but you had gone. What's the idea, hiding out on me?"

"Oh, I've been working."

One minute later I was in a big chair in front of the fire, with a bottle of the white port I had always liked beside me, a little pile of buttered English biscuits beside that, he was across from me with those long legs of his hooked over the chandelier or some place, and we were off. Or anyhow, he was. He always began in the middle, and he raced along about Don Giovanni, about an appoggiatura I was leaving out in Lucia, about the reason the old scores aren't sung the way they're written, about a new flutist he had pulled in from Detroit, about my cape routine in Carmen, all jumbled up together. But not for long. He got to the point pretty quick. "What's this about Hollywood?"

"Just what I told you. I'm sewed on a goddam contract and I've got to go."

I told him about it. I had told so many people about it by then I knew it by heart, and could get it over quick. "Then this man—Gold, did you say his name was?—is the key to the whole thing?"

"He's the one."

"All right then. You just sit here a while."

"No, if you're doing something I'll go!"

"I said sit there. Papa's going to get busy."

"At what?"

"There's your port, there's your biscuits, there's the fire, there's the most beautiful snow I've seen this year, and I've got the six big Rossini overtures on the machine —Semiramide, Tancred, the Barber, Tell, the Ladra, and the Italians, just in from London, beautifully played—and by the time they're finished I'll be back."

"I asked you, where are you going?"

"Goddam it, do you have to bust up my act? I'm being Papa. I'm going into action. And when Papa goes into action, it's the British Fleet. Sip your port. Listen to Rossini. Think of the boys that were gelded to sing the old bastard's masses. Be the Pope. I'm going to be Admiral Dewey."

"Beatty."

"No, I'm Bridley. I'm ready to fire."

He switched on the Rossini, poured the wine, and went. I tried to listen, and couldn't. I got up and switched it off. I was the first time I ever walked out on Rossini. I went over to the windows and watched the snow. Something told me to get out of there, to go back to Hollywood, to do anything except get mixed up with him again. It wasn't over twenty minutes before he was back. I heard him coming, and ducked back to the chair. I didn't want him to see me worrying. ". . . I was astonished that you missed that grace note in Lucia. Didn't you *feel* it there? Didn't you know it *had* to be there?"

"To hell with Lucia. What news?"

"Oh. I had forgotten all about it. Why, you stay, of

course. You go on with the opera, you do this foolish broadcast you've let yourself in for, you sing for me, you make your picture in the summer. That's all. It's all fixed up. Once more, Jack, on all those old recitatives—"

"Listen, this is business. I want to know—"

"Jack, you are so crass. Can't I wave my wand? Can't I do my bit of magic? If you have to know, I happen to control a bank, or my somewhat boorish family happen to control it. They embarrass me greatly, but sometimes they have a kind of low, swinish usefulness. And the bank controls, through certain stocks impounded to secure moneys, credit, and so on—oh the hell with it."

"Go on. The bank controls what?"

"The picture company, dolt."

"And?"

"Listen, I'm talking about Donizetti."

"And I'm talking about a son-of-a-bitch by the name of Rex Gold. What did you do?"

"I talked with him."

"And what did he say?"

"Why—I don't know. Nothing. I didn't wait to hear what he had to say. I told him what he was to do, that's all."

"Where's your phone?"

"Phone? What are you phoning about?"

"I've got to call the broadcasting company."

"Will you sit down and listen to what I'm trying to tell you about appoggiaturas, so you won't embarrass me every time you sing something written before 1905? Varlets in the bank are calling the broadcasting company. That's what we have them for. They're working overtime, calling other varlets in Radio City and making them work overtime, which I greatly enjoy, while you and I take our sinful ease here and watch the snow at twilight, and discuss the grace notes of Donizetti, which will be sung long after the picture company, the bank, and the varlets are dead in their graves and forgotten. Are you following me?"

His harangue on the appoggiaturas lasted fifteen minutes. It was something I was always forgetting about him, his connection with money. His family consisted of an old maid sister, a brother that was a colonel in the Illinois

National Guard, another brother that lived in Italy, and some nephews and nieces, and they had about as much to do with that fortune as so many stuffed dummies. He ran it, he controlled the bank, he did plenty of other things that he pretended he was too artistic even to bother with. All of a sudden something shot through my mind. "Winston, I've been framed."

"Framed? What are you talking about? By whom?"

"By you."

"Jack, I give you my word, the way you sang that—"

"Cut out this goddam foolish act about Lucia, will you? Sure I sang it wrong. I learned that role before I knew anything about style, and I hadn't sung it for five years until I went on with it last month, and I neglected to re-learn it, and that's all that amounts to, and to hell with it. I'm talking about this other. You knew all about it when you called me."

". . . Why, of course I did."

"And I think you put me in that spot."

"I—? Don't be a fool."

"It always struck me pretty funny, that guy Gold's ideas about grand opera, and me, and all the rest of it. Anybody else would *want* me in grand opera, to build me up. What do you know about that?"

"Jack, that's Mexican melodrama."

"What about this trip of yours? To Mexico?"

"I went there. A frightful place."

"For me?"

"Of course."

"Why?"

"To take you by the scuff of your thick neck and drag you out of there. I—ran into a 'cellist that had seen you. I heard you were looking seedy. I don't like you seedy. Shaggy, but not with spots on your coat."

"What about Gold?"

" . . . I put Gold in charge of that picture company because he was the worst ass I had ever met, and I thought he was the perfect man to make pictures. I was right. He's turned the whole investment into a gold mine. Soon I can have seventy-five men, and 'Little Orchestra' will be one of those affectations I so greatly enjoy. Jack, do you have to expose all my little shams? You know them all. Can't we just not look at them? After all they're nice shams."

"I want to know more about Gold."

He came over and sat on the arm of my chair. "Jack, why should I frame you?"

I couldn't answer him, and I couldn't look at him.

"Yes, I knew all about it. I didn't tell Gold to be an ass, if that's what you mean. I didn't have to. I knew about it, and I acted out one of my little shams. Can't I want my Jack to be happy? Wipe that sulky look off your face. Wasn't it good magic? Didn't Gridley level the fort?"

"... Yes."

I got home around eight o'clock. I rushed in with a grin on my face, said it was all right, that Gold had changed his mind, that we were going to stay, and let's go out and celebrate. She got up, wiped her snoddy nose, dressed, and we went out, to a hot-spot uptown. It was murder to drag her out, on a night like that, the way she felt, but I was afraid if I didn't get to some place where there was music, and I could get some liquor in me, she'd see I was putting on an act, that I was as jittery inside as a man with a hangover.

I didn't see him for a week or ten days, and the first broadcast made me feel good. I said hello to Captain Conners, and there was a federal kick-back the next morning. Messages to private persons are strictly forbidden. I just laughed, and thought of Thomas. There was a federal kick-back on that "Good night, Mother," too, and they told him he couldn't do it. He just went ahead and did it. That afternoon there came a radiogram from the SS. *Port of Cobh:* TWAS A SOAP AGENTS PROGRAM BUT I ENJOYED IT HELLO YOURSELF AND HELLO TO THE LITTLE ONE CONNERS. So of course I had to come running home with that.

I made some records, went on three times a week at the opera, did another broadcast, and woke up to find I was a household institution, name, face, voice and all, from

Hudson Bay to Cape Horn and back again. The spig papers, the Canadian papers, the Alaskan papers, and all the other papers began coming in by that time, and I was plastered all over them, with reviews of the broadcast, pictures of the car, and pictures of me. The plugs I wrote for the car worked, the horn worked, and all of it worked, so they had to put more ships under charter to make deliveries. Then I had to get Winston's program ready, and began seeing him every day.

I didn't have to see him every day to get the program up. But he dropped into my dressing room one night, the way he had done before, and it was just luck that it was raining, and she still had a hangover from the cold, and had decided to stay home. She was generally out there when I sang, and always came backstage to pick me up. There was a big mob of autograph hunters back there, and instead of locking them out while I dressed, the way I generally did, I let them in, and signed everything they shoved at me, and listened to women tell me how they had come all the way from Aurora to hear me, and let him wait. When we walked out I apologized for it and said there was nothing I could do. "Don't ever come around again. This isn't Paris. Let me drop up to your hotel the morning after, and we'll have the post-mortem then."

"I'd love it! It's a standing date."

From the quick way he said it, and the fact that he had never once asked me where I was living, or made any move to come and see me, it came to me that he knew all about Juana, just like he had known all about Gold. Then I began to have this nervous feeling, that never left me, wondering what he was going to pull next.

What I was going to do with her the night of his concert I didn't know. She had got so she could read the papers now, and had spotted the announcement, and asked me about it. I acted like it was just another job of singing, and she didn't pay much attention to it. Her cold was all right now, and there wasn't a chance she would stay home on that account. I thought of telling her it was a private concert, and that I couldn't get her in, but I knew

129

that wouldn't work. Going up in the cab, I told her that as I wouldn't have to dress afterwards, it would be better if she didn't come backstage. We'd meet in the Russian place next door. Then I could duck out quick and we'd miss the mob of handshakers. I showed it to her and she said all right, then she went in the front way and I ducked up the alley.

When I got backstage I almost fainted when I found out what he was up to. I was singing two numbers, one the aria from the Siege of Corinth for the first part of the program, the other Walter Damrosch's Mandalay, for the second part. I had squawked on that Mandalay, because I thought it was all wrong for a symphony concert. But when he made me read it over I had to admit it was in a different class from the Speaks Mandalay, or the Prince Mandalay, or any of the other barroom Mandalays. It's a little tone poem all by itself, a piece of real music, with all the verses in it except the bad one, about the house-maids, and each verse a little different from the others. One reason it's never done is that it takes a whole male chorus, but of course cost never bothered him any. He got a chorus together, and rehearsed them until they spit blood, getting a Volga-Boat-Song-dying-away effect he wanted at the end, and by the time I had gone over it with them two or three times, we had a real number out of it.

But what he was getting ready to do was have them march on in a body, before I came on, and I had to throw a fit of temperament to stop it. I raved and cursed, said it would kill my entrance, and refused to go on if he did it that way. I said they had to drift in with the orchestra after the intermission, and take their places without any march-on. But I wasn't thinking about my entrance. What I was afraid of was that those twenty-four chorus men, marching on at a Winston Hawes concert, would be such a murderous laugh that it would tip her off to what the whole thing was about.

I peeped out before we started, and spotted her. She was

sitting between an old couple, on one side, and one of the critics, alone, on the other, so it didn't look like she would hear anything. In the intermission I peeped out again. She was still sitting there, and so was the old couple. She had sneaked a piece of chewing gum into her mouth, and was munching on that, so everything seemed to be all right, so far.

The chorus were in white ties, and they went on the way I said, and nothing happened. The orchestra played a number and Winston came off. He kidded me about my fit of temperament, and I kidded back. So long as everything was under control, I didn't care. Then I went on. Whether it was what Damrosch wrote, or the way Winston conducted, or the tone of those horns, I don't know, but before the opening chords had even finished, you were in India. I started, and did a good job of it. I clowned the second verse a little, but not too much. The other verses I did straight, and the temple-bell atmosphere kept getting better. When we got to the end, with the chorus dying away behind me, and me hanging above them on the high F, it was something to hear, believe me it was. They broke out into a roar. It had been a program of modern music, most of it pretty scrappy and this was the first thing they had heard that really stuck to their ribs. I took two calls, had the chorus stand, came off, and they called me out again. Then Winston did something that's not done, and that he wouldn't have done for anybody on earth but me. He decided to repeat it.

A repeat is something you do mechanically, God knows why. You've done it once, you've scored with it, and the second time out you do it with your mouth, but your head has already gone home. I went through with it, got every laugh I had got before, coasted along without a hitch. I hit the E flat, the chorus was right with me. I hit the F, and my heart stopped. Hanging up there, over that chorus, was the priest of Acapulco, the guy in the church, singing down the storm, croaking high mass to make the face on the cross stop looking at him.

"Who is these man?"

We were in the cab going down, and it was like the whisper you hear from a coiled rattlesnake.

"What man?"

"I think you know, yes."

"I don't even know what you're talking about."

"You have been with a man."

"I've been with plenty of men. I see men all day long. Do I have to stay with you all the time? What the hell are you talking about?"

"I no speak of man you see all day long. I speak of man you love. Who is these man?"

"Oh, I'm a fairy, is that it?"

"Yes."

"Well, thanks. I didn't know that."

It was a warm night, but on account of the white tie I had to wear a coat. I had been hot as hell going up, but I wasn't hot now. I felt cold and shriveled inside. I watched the El posts going by on Third Avenue, and I could feel her there looking at me, looking at me with those hard black eyes that seemed to bore through me. We got out of the cab, and went on up to the apartment. I put the silk hat in a closet, put the coat in with it, lit a cigarette, tried to shake it off, how I felt. She just sat there on the edge of the table. She had on an evening dress we had got from one of the best shops in town, and the bullfighter's cape. Except for the look on her face, she was something out of a book.

"Why you lie to me?"

"I'm not lying."

"You lie. I look at you, I know you lie."

"Did I ever lie to you?"

"Yes. Once at Acapulco. You know you run away, you tell me no. When you want, you lie."

"We went over that. I meant to run away, and you knew what I meant. Lying, that was just how we got over it easy. Then when I found out what you meant to me, I didn't lie. That's all . . . what the hell squwk have you got? You were all ready to sleep with that son-of-a-bitch—"

"I no lie."

132

"What has this got to do with Acapulco?"

"Yes, it is the same. Now you love man, you lie."

"I don't—Christ, do I look like that?"

"No. You no look like that. We meet in Tupinamba, yes? And you no look like that. I like, much, how you look. Then you make *lotería* for me, and lose *lotería*. And I think, how sweet. He have lose, but he like me so much he make *lotería*. Then I send muchacha with address, and we go home, go where I live. But then I know. You know how I know?"

"Don't know, don't care. It's not true."

"I know when you sing. Hoaney, I was street girl, love man, three pesos. Little dumb muchacha, no can read, no can write, understand nothing like that. But of man—all. . . . Hoaney, these man who love other man, they can do much, very clever. But no can sing. Have no toro in high voice, no grrr that frighten little muchacha, make heart beat fast. Sound like old woman, like cow, like priest."

She began to walk around. My hands were clammy and my lips felt numb. ". . . Then the político, he say I should open house, and I think of you. I think maybe, with these man, no like muchacha, have no trouble. We got to Acapulco. Rain come, we go in church. You take me. I no want, I think of sacrilegio, but you take me. Oh, much toro. I like. I think maybe Juana make mistake. Then you sing, oh, my heart beat very fast."

"Just a question of toro, hey?"

"No. You ask me come with you. I come. I love you much. I no think of toro. Just a little bit. Then in New York I feel, I feel something fonny. I think you think about contrato, all these thing. But is not the same. To-night I know. I make no mistake. When you love Juana, you sing nice, much toro. When you love man—why you lie to me? You think I no hear? You think I no know?"

If she had taken a whip to me I couldn't have answered her. She began to cry, and fought it back. She went in the other room, and pretty soon she came out. She had changed her dress and put on a hat. She was carrying the valise in one hand and the fur coat in the other. "I no live with man who love other man. I no live with man who lie. I—"

133

The phone rang. "—Ah!"

She ran in and answered. "Yes, he is here."

She came out, her eyes blazing and her white teeth showing behind something that was between a laugh and a snarl. "Mr. Hawes."

I didn't say anything and I didn't move. "Yes, Mr. Hawes, the director." She gave a rasping laugh and put on the goddamdest imitation of Winston you ever saw, the walk, the stick, and all the rest of it so you almost thought he was in front of you. "Yes, your sweetie, he wait at telephone, talk to him please."

When I still sat there, she jumped at me like a tiger, shook me till I could feel my teeth rattling, and then ran in to the telephone. "What you want with Mr. Sharp, please? . . . Yes, yes, he will come. . . . Yes, thank you much. Goodbye."

She came out again. "Now, please you go. He have party, want you very much. Now, go to your sweetie. Go! Go! Go!"

She shook me again, jerked me out of the chair, tried to push me out the door. She grabbed up the valise and the fur coat again. I ran in the bedroom, flopped on the bed, pulled the pillow over my head. I wanted to shut it out, the whole horrible thing she had showed me, where she had ripped the cover off my whole life, dragged out what was down there all the time. I screwed my eyes shut, kept pulling the pillow around my ears. But one thing kept slicing up at me, no matter what I did. It was the fin of that shark.

I don't know how long I stayed there. I was on my back after a while, staring at nothing. It was dead quiet outside, and dead still, except for the searchlight from the building on Fourteenth Street, that kept going around and around. I kept telling myself she was crazy, that voice is a matter of palate, sinus, and throat, that Winston had no more to do with what happened to me in Paris than the scenery had. But here it was, starting on me again the same way it had before, and I knew she had called it on me the way it was written in the big score, and that no pillow or anything else could shut it out. I closed my eyes, and I was going down under the waves, with something coming up at me from below. Panic caught me then. I hadn't heard her go out, and I called her. I waited, and called again. There wasn't any answer. My head was under the pillow again pretty soon, and I must have slept because I woke up with the same horrible dream, that I was in the water, going down, and this thing was coming at me. I sat up, and there she was, on the edge of her bed, looking at me. It was gray outside. "Christ, you're there." But some kind of a sob jerked out as I said it, and I put out my hand and took hers.

"It's all true."

She came over, sat down beside me, stroked my hair, held my hand. "Tell me. You no lie, I no fight."

"There's nothing to tell. . . . Every man has got five per cent of that in him, if he meets the one person that'll bring it out, and I did, that's all."

"But you love other man. Before."

"No, the same one, here, in Paris, all over, the one son-of-a-bitch that's been the curse of my life."

"Sleep now. Tomorrow, you give me little bit money, I go back to Mexico—"

"No! Don't you know what I'm trying to tell you? That's out! I hate it! I've been ashamed of it, I've tried to shake it off, I hoped you would never find out, and now it's over!"

I was holding her to me. She began stroking my hair again, looking down in my eyes. "You love me, Hoaney?"

"Don't you know it? Yes. If I never said so, it was just because—did we have to say it? If we felt it, wasn't that a hell of a sight more?"

All of a sudden she broke from me, shoved the dress down from her shoulder, slipped the brassiere and shoved a nipple in my mouth. "Eat. Eat much. Make big *toro!*"

"I know now, my whole life comes from there."

"Yes, eat."

11

WE DIDN'T GET UP for two days, but it wasn't like the time we had in the church. We didn't get drunk and we didn't laugh. When we were hungry, we'd call up the French restaurant down the street and have them send something in. Then we'd lie there and talk, and I'd tell her more of it, until it was all off my chest and I had nothing more to say. Once I quit lying to her, she didn't seem surprised, or shocked, or anything like that. She would look at me, with her eyes big and black, and nod, and sometimes say something that made me think she understood a lot more about it than I did, or most doctors do. Then I'd take her in my arms, and afterward we'd sleep, and I felt a peace I hadn't felt for years. All those awful jitters of that last few weeks were gone, and sometimes when she was asleep and I wasn't, I'd think about the Church, and confession, and what it must mean to people that have something lying heavy on their soul. I had left the Church before I had anything on my soul, and the confession business, to me then, was just a pain in the neck. But I understood it now, understood a lot of things I had never understood before. And mostly I understood what a woman could mean to a man. Before, she had been a pair of eyes, and a shape, something to get excited about. Now, she seemed something to lean on, and draw something from, that nothing else could give me. I thought of books I had read, about worship of the earth, and how she was always called Mother, and none of it made much sense, but those big round breasts did, when I put my head on them, and they began to tremble, and I began to tremble.

The morning of the second day we heard the church

bells ringing, and I remembered I was due to sing at the Sunday night concert. I got up, went to the piano, and tossed a few high ones around. I was just trying them out, but I didn't have to. They were like velvet. At six o'clock we dressed, had a little something to eat, and went down there. I was in a Rigoletto excerpt, from the second act, with a tenor, a bass, a soprano, and a mezzo that were all getting spring try-outs. I was all right. When we got home we changed to pajamas again, and I got out the guitar. I sang her the Evening Star song, Träume, Schmerzen, things like that. I never liked Wagner, and she couldn't understand a word of German. But it had earth, rain, and the night in it, and went with the humor we were in. She sat there with her eyes closed, and I sang it half voice. Then I took her hand and we sat there, not moving.

A week went by, and still I didn't see Winston. He must have called twenty times, but she took all calls, and when it was him she would just say I wasn't in, and hang up. I had nothing to say to him but goodbye, and I wasn't going to say that, because I didn't want to play the scene. Then one day, after we had been out for breakfast, we stepped out of the elevator, and there he was at the end of the hall, watching porters carrying furniture into an apartment. He looked at us and blinked, then dived at us with his hand out. "Jack! Is that you? Well, of all the idiotic coincidences!"

I felt my blood freeze for fear of what she was going to do, but she didn't do anything. When I happened not to see his hand, he began waving it around, and kept chattering about the coincidence, about how he had just signed a lease for an apartment in this very building, and here we were. She smiled. "Yes, very fonny."

There didn't seem to be anything to do but introduce him, so I did. She held out her hand. He took it and bowed. He said he was happy to know her. She said gracias, she had been at his concert, and she was honored to know him. Two beautiful sets of manners met in the hall that day, and it seemed queer, the venom that was back of them.

The door of the freight elevator opened, and more furniture started down the hall. "Oh, I'll have to show them where to put it. Come in, you two, and have a look at my humble abode."

"Some other time, Winston, we—"

"Yes, gracias, I like."

We went in there, and he had one of the apartments on the south tier, the biggest in the building, with a living room the size of a recital hall, four or five bedrooms and baths, servants' rooms, study, everything you could think of. The stuff I remembered from Paris was there, rugs, tapestries, furniture, all of it worth a fortune, and a lot of things I had never seen. Four or five guys in denim suits were standing around, waiting to be told where to put their loads. He paid no attention to them, except to direct them with one hand, like they were a bunch of bull fiddlers. He sat us down on a sofa, pulled up a chair for himself, and went on talking about how he was sick of hotel living, had about given up all hope of finding an apartment he liked, and then had found this place, and then of all the cock-eyed things, here we were.

Or were we? I said yes, we were at the other end of the hall. We all laughed: He started in on Juana, asked if she wasn't Mexican. She said yes, and he started off about his trip there, and what a wonderful country it was, and I had to hand it to him he had found out more about it in a week than I had in six months. You would have thought he might have conveniently left out what he went down there for. He didn't. He said he went down there to bring me back. She laughed, and said she saw me first. He laughed. That was the first time there was the least little glint in their eyes.

"Oh, I must show you my cricket!"

He jumped up, grabbed a hatchet, and began chopping a small crate apart. Then he lifted out a block of pink stone, a little bigger than a football and about the same shape, but carved and polished into the form of a cricket, with its legs drawn up under it and its head huddled between its front feet. She made a little noise and began to finger it.

138

"Look at that, Jack. Isn't it marvelous? Pure Aztec, at least five hundred years old. I brought it back from Mexico with me, and I'd hate to tell you what I had to do to get it out of the country. Look at that simplification of detail. If Manship had done it, they'd have thought it was a radical sample of his work. The line of that belly is pure Brancusi. It's as modern as a streamlined plane, and yet some Indian did it before he even saw a white man."

"Yes, yes. Make me feel very nostálgica."

Then came the real Hawes touch. He picked it up, staggered with it over to the fireplace, and put it down. "For my hearth!"

She got up to go, and I did. "Well, children, you know now where I live, and I want to be seeing a lot of you."

"Yes, gracias."

"And oh! As soon as I'm moved in, I'm giving a little housewarming, and you're surely coming to it—"

"Well, I don't know, Winston, I'm pretty busy—"

"Too busy for my housewarming? Jack, Jack, Jack!"

"Gracias, Señor Hawes. Perhaps we come."

"Perhaps? Certainly you'll come!"

I was plenty shaky when we got to our own apartment. "Listen, Juana, we're getting out of this dump, and we're getting out quick. I don't know what the hell his game is, but this is no coincidence. He's moved in on us, and we're going to beat it."

"We beat it, he come too."

"Then we'll beat it again. I don't want to see him."

"Why you run away?"

"I don't know. It—makes me nervous. I want to be somewhere where I don't have to see him, don't have to think of him, don't have to feel that he's around."

"I think we stay."

We saw him twice more that day. Once, around six o'clock, he rang the buzzer and asked us to dinner, but I was singing and said we would have to eat later. Then, some time after midnight, when we had got home, he dropped in with a kid named Pudinsky, a Russian pianist that was to play at his next concert. He said they were

139

going to run over some stuff, and for us to come on down. We said we were tired. He didn't argue. He put his arm around Pudinsky, and they left. While we were undressing we could hear the piano going. The kid could play all right.

"I see his game now."

"Yes. Very fonny game."

"That boy. I'm supposed to get jealous."

"Are you jealous?"

"No. Jealous—what the hell are you talking about? What difference does it make to me what he does, once I'm out of it? But it makes me nervous. I—I wish he was somewhere else. I wish we were all somewhere else."

She lay there for a long time, up on one elbow, looking down at me. Then she kissed me and went over to her own bed. It was daylight before I got to sleep.

Next day he was in and out half a dozen times, and the day after that, and that day after that. I began missing cues, the first sign you get that you're not right. The voice was in shape, and I was getting across, but the prompter began throwing the finger at me. It was the first time in my life that that had ever happened.

In about a week came the invitation to the housewarming. I tried to beg out of it, said I had to sing that night, but she smiled and said gracias, we would go, and he put his arm around her and you would have thought they were pals, but I knew them both like a book, and could tell there was something back of it, on both sides. After he left I got peevish and wanted to know why the hell she was shoving me into it all the time. "Hoaney, with this man, it do you no good to run away. He see you no care, then maybe he estop. He know you have afraid, he never estop. We go. We laugh, have fine time, no care . . . You care?"

"For God's sake, no."

"I think yes, little bit. I think we have—how you say— the goat."

"He's got my goat all right, but not for that reason. I just don't want any more to do with him."

"Then you care. Maybe not so, how he want. But you have afraid. When you no care at all, he estop. Now—we no run away. We go, you sing, be fine fallow, no give a damn. And you watch, will be all right."

"If I have to, I have to, but Christ, I hate it."

So we went. I was singing Faust, and I was so lousy I almost did get stuck in the duel scene. But I was washed up by ten thirty, and we came home and dressed. It wasn't any white dress with flowers on it this time. She put on a bottle-green evening dress, and over that the bullfighter's cape, and that embroidered crimson and yellow silk, sliding over the green taffeta, made a rustle you could hear coming, I'm here to tell you, and all those colors, over the light copper of her skin, was a picture you could look at. I put on a white tie, but no overcoat or anything, and about a quarter after eleven we stepped out and walked down the hall.

When we got in there, the worst drag was going on you ever saw in your life. A whole mob of them was in there, girls in men's evening clothes tailored for them, with shingle haircuts and blue make-up in their eyes, dancing with other girls dressed the same way, young guys with lipstick on, and mascara eyelashes, dancing with each other too, and at least three girls in full evening dress, that you had to look at twice to make sure they weren't girls at all. Pudinsky was at the piano, but he wasn't playing Brahms. He was playing jazz. The whole thing made me sick to my stomach as soon as I looked at it, but I swallowed hard and tried to act like I was glad to be there.

Winston had on a purple velvet dinner coat with a silk sash knotted around it, and he brought us in like it was all for us. He introduced us, and got us drinks, and Pudinsky slammed into the Pagliacci Prologue, and I stepped up and sang it, and clowned it with as good a grin as I could get on my face. While they were still clapping, Winston turned around and began to throw the show to Juana. She still hadn't taken off the cape, and he lifted it off her shoulders, and began going into a spasm about it. They all crowded up to look, and when he found out it was a real bullfighter's cape, nothing would suit him but that she had to tell them all about the fine points of bull-fighting. I sat down, and got this feeling it wasn't on the up-and-up, that something was coming. I thought of Chadwick, and wondered if this was another play to show her up. But that wasn't it. Except that Winston would put his arm around Pudinsky every time he saw me looking at him, he didn't pull anything. He put her in the spot, and made her explain the whole routine of bull-fighting, and she took the cape to show them, and she was pretty funny, and so was he. Nobody could make a woman look good better than Winston, when he wanted to. Pretty soon somebody yelled out: "How the hell does a man study to be a bullfighter, that's what I want to know."

Winston went down on his knees in front of Juana.

"Yes, will you tell us that? Just what are the practice exercises for a bullfighter?"

"Oh, I explain you."

They all sat down, and Winston squatted at her feet.

"First, the little boy, he wants to be a bullfighter, yes? All little boy want to be bullfighter."

"I always did. I do still."

"So, I tell you how you do. You find nice burro, you know what is burro?"

"A little jackass, something like that?"

"Yes. You get little jackass, you cut two big maguey leaf, you know maguey, yes? Have big leaf, much thick, much sharp—?"

"Century plant?"

"Yes. Tie leaf on head of little jackass, make big horn, like bull—"

"Wait a minute."

Some woman dug up a ribbon, and Winston broke off fronds from a fern, and with the ribbon and the fern leaves, he stuck the horns on his head. Then he got down on his hands and knees in front of Juana. "Go on."

"Yes, just so. You look much like little jackass."

That got a shout. Winston looked up, kicked his heels, and let out a jackass bellow. It was a little funnier than it sounds.

"Then you get little stick, for *espada*, and little red rag, for *muleta*, and practice with little jackass." Somebody dug up a silver-headed cane, and she took it, and the cape, and the two of them began doing a bullfight act in the middle of the floor. The rest of them were screeching and yelling by that time, and I was sitting there, wondering what the hell was up. The buzzer sounded. Somebody went to the door, came back, and touched me on the arm. "Telegram for you, Mr. Sharp."

I went out in the hall.

Harry, one of the bellboys, was out there, and shoved a telegram at me. I opened it. It was nothing but a blank form shoved in an envelope. "Is the messenger still there? He's given you nothing but a blank."

Harry closed the door to the apartment. You could still hear them in there, screeching over the bullfight. "Let me talk quick, Mr. Sharp, so you can get back in there before anybody thinks anything. I had to have a telegram in my hand, so it would look right. . . . There's a man down there, waiting for you. I told him you were out. He went up to your apartment, then he came down again, and he's down there now."

"In the lobby?"

"Yes sir."

"What does he want?"

". . . Mr. Sharp, Tony put through three calls today for this new party, Mr. Hawes. They were all to the immigration service. Tony remembered the number from a year ago, when his brother came from Italy. Tony thinks this man is a federal, come to take Miss Montes away."

"Is Tony on?"

"We're both on. Get back in there, Mr. Sharp, before this Hawes gets tipped off. Get her out of there, and have her press the elevator button twice. Either me or Tony will get her out through the basement, and then you can stall this guy till she gets under cover. Tony thinks his people will take her in. They're fans of yours."

I had a wad of money in my pocket. I took it out and peeled off a ten. "Split that with Tony. There'll be more tomorrow. She'll be right down."

"Yes, sir."

"And thanks. More thanks than I know how to say."

I stepped back in. I took care to be stuffing the telegram in my pocket as I came. Winston jumped up from where he was still galumphing around the floor, and came over. "What is it, Jack?"

"Just some greetings from Hollywood."

"Bad?"

"Little bit."

"Well, what is it? By God, I'd love to wake the sons-of-bitches up and tell them where they get off."

"Wouldn't wake them up, that's the trouble. It's only ten o'clock there. To hell with it, I'll tell you later. And to hell with bullfighting. Let's dance."

"Dance we shall. Hey, professor—music!"

Pudinsky began to bat out more jazz, they grabbed each other, and I grabbed Juana. "Now get a grin on your face. I've got something to tell you."

"Yes, here is nice grin."

I laid it out for her fast. "This Pudinsky thing is nothing but a smoke screen. He's turned in an anonymous tip against you, then you're to be taken to Ellis Island, then I'm to run to him for help, then he's to move heaven and earth—and fail. You're to be sent back to Mexico—"

"And then he gets you."

"So he thinks."

"So I think, too."

"Will you for God's sake stop that and—"

"Why you tremble?"

"I'm plenty scared of him, that's why. Now listen—"

"Yes, I listen."

"Get out of here, quick. Get out on some stall so he thinks you're coming back. Change your dress, pack, as fast as you can. If the buzzer rings, keep still and don't answer. Go to the elevator, ring twice, and the boys will take care of you. Don't call me. Tomorrow I'll reach you through Tony. Here's some money."

I had palmed the wad, and slipped it down the back of her dress. "And once more, step on it!"

144

"Yes, I step."

She went over to Winston. He was sitting with Pudinsky, the fern leaves still in his hair. "You want to play *real* bullfight, yes?"

"I just thirst for it."

"Wait. I get things. I come back."

He showed her out, then came over to me. "Lovely girl."

"Yeah, she's all of that."

"I've always said there were two nations under every flag, male and female. I wouldn't give a damn for all the Mexican men that ever lived, but the women are marvelous. What saps their painters are, with all that beauty around them, to spend their days on war, socialism, and politics. Mexican art is nothing but a collection of New Masses covers."

"Whatever it is, I don't like it."

"Who would? But if they could paint her face, that would have been different. Goya could have, but those worthy radicals, no. Well—they don't know what they miss."

I went over, sat down and watched them dance. They were getting lit by now, and it was pretty raw. I wished I had fixed up some signal from the boys, so I would know when she was out. I hadn't, so all I could do was sit there. I was going to wait till he missed her, then go down to the apartment to find her, then come back and say she didn't feel well, and had gone to bed. It would all take time, give her a start, but I had to take the play from him.

I had looked at my watch when she went. It was seven after one. After a hell of a time I slipped back to a bathroom and looked again. It was eleven after. She had been gone four minutes: I came back and sat down again. Pudinsky stopped and they all yelled for more. He said he was tired. The buzzer rang. Winston opened, and I began thinking of a stall in case it was the detective. Who stepped in was Juana. She hadn't changed her dress. Over her arm was the cape, in one hand was the *espada*, and in the other the ear.

They had got a little sick of bullfighting, but when they

saw the ear they began to yell again. They passed it around, and felt it, and smelled it, and say "Peyooh!" Winston took it, held it up to his head and wobbled it, and they laughed and clapped. He got down on the floor again and bellowed. Juana laughed. "Yes, now you are no more jackass. Big bull."

He bellowed again. I was getting so nervous I was twitching. I went over to her. "Take that stuff back. I'm fed up on bullfighting, and that ear stinks. Take it back where you got it, and—"

I grabbed for the ear. Winston dodged. She laughed and wouldn't look at me. Something hit me in the belly. When I looked around I saw that one of the fags in woman's clothes had poked me with a broomstick. "Out of my way! I'm a picador! I'm a picador on his old white horse!"

Two or three more of them ran back and got broomsticks, or mops handles, or whatever was there, to be picadors, and began galloping around Winston, poking at him. Every time they touched him he'd bellow. Juana drew the espada, and spread the cape with it, like it was a muleta. Winston began charging it, on one hand and his knees, still holding the ear with his other hand and wobbling it. Pudinsky began to rip off the bullring music from Carmen. There was so much noise you couldn't even hear yourself think. I walked over and leaned on the piano, with my back to it, till she would get the clowning over and I would have another chance to get her out.

All of a sudden Pudinsky stopped, and this "Ooh!" went around the room. I turned around. She was standing there, like a statue, the way they do for the kill, with her left side to Winston, the sword in her right hand, up at the level of her eyes, and pointing right at him. In her left hand, down in front of him, she held the cape. He was down there looking at it, and wobbling the ear at it. Pudinsky began to play blue chords on the piano.

Winston snorted a couple of times, then looked up at her, like he wanted a cue on what to do next. Then he jumped up, and back, but a sofa caught him. A man yelled. I jumped for the sword arm, but I was too late. That esapada thrust isn't something in slow motion, like you maybe have thought from reading the books. It goes like lightning, and next thing I knew the point of the steel was sticking out the back of the sofa, and blood was foaming out of Winston's mouth, and she was over him, talking to him, laughing at him, telling him the detective was waiting to take him down to hell.

It flashed over me, that mob at the novelladas, pouring down out of the *sol*, twisting the tail of the dying bull, yelling at him, kicking at him, spitting on him, and I tried to tell myself I had hooked up with a savage, that it was horrible. It was no use. I wanted to laugh, and cheer, and yell *Olé!* I knew I was looking at the most magnificent thing I had ever seen in my life.

12

SHE SPIT INTO THE BLOOD, stepped back, and picked up the cape. For a second all you could hear was Pudinsky, over at the piano, gasping and slobbering in an agony of fright. Then they made a rush for the door, to get out before the police came. They fought to get past each other, the women cursing like men, the fags screaming like women, and when they got to the hall they didn't wait for the elevator. They went piling down the stairway, and some of them fell, and you could hear more curses, and screams, and thuds, where they were kicking each other. She came over and knelt beside me, where I had folded into a chair. "Now, he no get. Goodbye, and remember Juana." She kissed me, jumped up, and rustled out. I sat there, still looking at that thing that was pinned to the sofa, with its head hanging over the back, and the blood drying on the shirt. Pudinsky lifted his head, where it was buried in his hands, saw it, let out a moan, and ran over to a corner, where he put his head down and broke out into more sobs. I picked up a rug to throw on it. Then something twisted in my stomach, and I stumbled back to a bathroom. I hadn't eaten since afternoon, but white stuff began coming up, and even after my stomach was empty it kept retching, and horrible sounds came out of me from the air it forced up. I saw my face in the mirror. It was green.

When I came out two cops were there, and four or five of the fags, and one of the girls in a dinner coat, and a guy in a derby hat. Whether he was the dick that had been waiting for Juana, and he grabbed some of them on the way out, I didn't know. When the cops saw me they motioned me to stand aside, and one of them went back to phone. Pretty soon two more cops came up, and a couple of detectives, and next thing, the place was full of cops. There was one guy that seemed to be a doctor, and another that seemed to be a police photographer. Anyway, he set up a tripod, and began setting off bulbs and throwing them in the fern pot. Pretty soon a cop went over, motioned to me, and he, a detective, and I went out. I didn't have any coat there, but I didn't say anything about it. I didn't know whether they had Juana, or even where she had gone, and I was afraid if I asked them to let me go to the apartment, they would come with me and find her. We went down in the elevator. Harry ran us down. When we got to the lobby, more cops were there, talking to Tony.

We got in a police car, drove down Second Avenue, then down Lafayette Street, and on downtown to a place that seemed to be police headquarters. We got out, went in, and the cops took me in a room and told me to sit down. One of them went out. The other stayed, and picked up an afternoon paper that was on the table. We must have sat an hour, he reading the paper and neither of us saying anything. After a while I asked him if he had a cigarette. He passed over a pack without looking up. I smoked and we sat for another hour. Outside it was beginning to get light.

About six o'clock a detective came in, sat down, and stared at me a while. Then he began to talk. "You was there tonight? At this here Hawes's place?"

"Yes, I was."

"You seen him killed?"

"I did."

"What she kill him for?"

"That I don't know."

"Come on, you know. What you trying to do, kid me?"

"I told you I don't know."

"You live with her?"

"Yes."

"Then what do you mean you don't know? What she kill him for."

"I've got no idea at all."

"Was she in this country illegal?"

I knew by that Tony had spilled what he knew. "That I can't tell you. She might have been."

"What the hell can you tell me?"

"Anything I know I'll tell you."

He roared for a minute about how he could make me tell him, but that was a mistake. It gave me time to think. That illegal entry was a way he could tie me in, and hold me if he wanted to, and I knew the only way I could be of any use to her was to get out of there. Whether they had got her or not I didn't know, but I couldn't be any good sitting behind bars. I kept looking at him, thinking over the entries on my passport, and by the time he began asking questions again I had it all in hand, and thought I could get away with a lie. "So you quit that goddam stalling. One more thing you can't tell me and I'll open you up. Come on. She was in illegal, wasn't she?"

"I told you I don't know."

"Did you bring her in?"

"I did not."

"What? Wasn't you in Mexico?"

"Yes, I was."

"Didn't you bring her in with you?"

"I did not. I met her in Los Angeles."

"How you come in?"

"I rode a bus up to Nogales, caught a ride to San Antonio, and from there took another bus to Los Angeles. I met her about a week after that, in the Mexican quarter. Then I began working for pictures, and we hooked up. Then she came with me to New York."

I saw I had led with my chin on that, on account of the white slave charge. He snapped it back at me before I even finished. "Oh, so you brought her to New York."

"I did not. She paid her own fare."

"What the hell are you trying to tell me? Didn't I say cut that stalling out?"

"All right, ask her."

Then came a flicker in his eye. I had a quick hunch they hadn't got her yet. "Ask her, that's all I've got to say. Don't be silly. I'm not paying any woman's fare from Los Angeles to New York. I heard of the Mann Act too."

"Who turned in the tip against her?"

"That I don't know."

"Come on—"

"I told you I don't know. Now if you'll cut out your goddam nonsense, I'll tell you what I do know, and maybe it'll help you out, I don't know. But you can just drop this third-degree stuff right now, or I'll be starting a little third-degree of my own before long that you may not like so well."

"What do you mean by that?"

"You know what I mean. You're not talking to some Hell's Kitchen gunman. I've got a few friends, see? I don't ask any favors. But I'm claiming my rights, and I'll get them."

"All right, Sharp. Shoot it."

"We went to the party, she and I."

"Yeah, that drag was a funny place for a guy like you."

"He was a pixie, but he was also a musician, and I had worked for him, and when he asked us to his house-warming—"

"Are you a pix?"

"Starting up again, are you?"

"Go on, Sharp. Just checking up."

150

"So we went. And pretty soon one of the boys came up, and—"

"One of them pixes?"

"One of the bellboys. And I found out there was a guy downstairs waiting to see me. And I found out Hawes had put in three calls that day to the Immigration Office—"

"Then he *did* turn her in?"

"I told you I don't know. I wasn't taking any chances. I told her what the boys had told me, and tried to get her out of there. I told her to leave, and she did, but then she came back with this sword, and they started up again this bullfight game they had been playing—"

"Yeah, we know all about that."

"And she let him have it. And goddam well he had it coming to him. What the hell business was it of his whether she—"

"What he turn her in for?"

"That I don't know either. He had tried to tell me once or twice that living with a girl the way we did wasn't doing me any good, that it was hurting my career—"

"Your singing career?"

"That's right."

"What he have to do with that?"

"He had plenty to do with it. I don't only sing here in New York. I'm under contract to a Hollywood picture company, and he controlled the picture company, or said he did, and he was afraid—"

"Hays office stuff?"

"That's it."

"Oh, I get it now. Go on."

"That's all. It wasn't just morals, take it from me it wasn't, or friendship, or anything like that. It was money, and fear that the Mann Act would ruin one of his big stars, and stuff like that. All right, he went up against the wrong person. She let him have it, and now let him count up his Class A preferred stock."

He asked me a few more questions and then went out. As near as I could tell I had done all right. I had fixed her up with a motive that anyway made sense, him trying to bust us up, and it would look a hell of a sight better after we were married, as I knew we would be before the case ever came to trial. I had kept out of it what was really between Winston and me. I would have even told him that if it would have done her any good, but I knew that one whisper of that would crack everything wide open, and ruin her. I had anyhow made some kind of a stall about the Mann Act and the illegal entry, and they couldn't disprove it unless she told them different, and I knew they'd never get anything out of her. Around seven o'clock they gave me something to eat, and I waited for their next move.

Around eight o'clock a cop came in with one of my traveling cases, with clothes in it. That meant they had been in the apartment. I was still in evening clothes, and began to change. "You got a washroom here?"

"O.K., we'll take you to it. You want a barber?"

All I had in my pocket, after giving her the money was silver, but I counted it. There were a couple of dollars of it. "Yeah, send him in."

He went out, and the cop that was guarding took me down to the washroom. There was a shower there, so I stripped, had a bath, and put on the other clothes. The barber came in and shaved me. I put the evening clothes in the traveling case. They had brought me a hat, and I put that on. Then we went back to the room we had left.

A little after nine I was still pounding on it in my mind, what I could do, and it came to me that one thing I could do was get a lawyer. I remembered Sholto. "I'd like to make a phone call. How about that?"

"You're allowed one call."

We went out in the hall, where there was a row of phones against the wall. I looked up Sholto's number, rang it, and got him on the line. "Oh hello, I was wondering if you'd call. I see you're in a little trouble."

"Yeah, and I want you."

"I'll be right down."

In about a half hour he showed up. He listened to me. About all I could tell him, with the cop sitting there, was that I wanted to get out, but that seemed to be all he wanted to know. "It's probably just a matter of bond."

"What am I held for? Do you know that?"

"Material witness."

"Oh, I see."

"As soon as I can see a bondsman—that is, unless you want to put up cash bond yourself."

"How much is it?"

"I don't know. At a guess, I'd say five thousand."

"Which way is quickest?"

"Oh, money talks."

He had a blank check, and I wrote out a check for ten thousand. "All right, that ought to cover it. I think we can get action in about an hour."

Around ten o'clock he was back, and he, and the cop, and I went over to court. It took about five minutes. An assistant district attorney was there, they set bail at twenty-five hundred, and after Sholto put it up, we went out and got in a cab. He passed over the rest of the cash, in hundred-dollar bills. I handed back ten of them. "Retainer."

"Very well, thanks."

The first thing I wanted to know was whether they had got her yet. When he said they hadn't, I grabbed an early afternoon paper a boy shoved in the window, and read it. It was smeared all over the front page, with my picture, and Winston's picture, but no picture of her. That was one break. As well as I could remember, she hadn't had any picture taken since she had been in the country. It was something we hadn't got around to. There was one story giving Winston's career, another telling about me, and a main story that told what had happened. Everything I had said to the detective was in there, and the big eight-column streamer called her the "Sword-Killer," and said she was "Sought." I was still reading when we pulled up at Radio City.

When we got up to his office I began going over what I had told the detective, the illegal entry stuff and all, and why I had said what I had, but pretty soon he stopped me. "Listen, get this straight. Your counsel is not your co-conspirator in deceiving the police. He's your representative at the bar, to see that you get every right that the law entitles you to, and that your case, or her case, or whatever case he takes, is presented as well as it can be. What you told the detective is none of my affair, and it's much better, at this time, that I know nothing of it. When the time comes, I'll ask for information, and you had better tell me the truth. But at the moment, I prefer not to know of any misrepresentation you've made. From now on, by the way, an excellent plan, in dealing with the police, would be to say nothing."

"I get it."

He kept walking around his office, then he picked up the paper and studied that a while, then walked around some more. "There's something I want to warn you about."

"Yeah. What?"

"It seemed to me I got you out very easily."

"I didn't do anything."

"If they had wanted to hold you, there were two or three charges, apparently, they could have brought against you. All bailable offenses, but they could have kept you there quite a while. They could have made trouble. Also, the bond was absurdly low."

"I don't quite follow you."

"They haven't got her. They may have her, tucked away in some station-house in the Bronx, they may be holding her there and saying nothing for fear of habeas corpus proceedings, but I don't think so. They haven't got her, and it's quite possible they've let you out so they can locate her through you."

"Oh, now I see what you mean."

"You going back to your apartment?"

"I don't know. I suppose so."

". . . You'll be watched. There'll probably be a tail on you day and night. Your phone may be tapped."

"Can they do that?"

"They can, and they do. There may be a dictaphone in there by now, and they're pretty good at thinking of places to put it without your finding it, or suspecting it.

It's a big apartment house, and that makes it all the easier for them. I don't know what her plans are, and apparently you don't. But it's a bad case. If they catch her, I'll do everything I can for her, but I warn you it's a bad case. It's much better that she not be located. . . . Be careful."

"I will."

"The big danger is that she phone you. Whatever you do, the second she rings up, warn her that she's being overheard."

"I'll remember that."

"You're being used as a decoy."

"I'll watch my step."

When I got up to Twenty-second Street a flock of reporters were there, and I stuck with them for about ten minutes. I thought it was better to answer their questions some kind of way, and get rid of them, than have them trying to get to me all day. When I got up to the apartment the phone was ringing, and a newspaper was on the line, offering me five thousand dollars for a signed story of what I knew about it, and about her, and I said no, and hung up. It started to ring again, and I flashed the board and told them not to put through any more incoming calls, or let anybody up. The door buzzer sounded. I answered, and it was Harry and Tony, on hand to tell me what they knew. I peeled off a hundred-dollar bill as they started to talk, handed it over, and then remembered about the dictaphone. We went out in the hall, and they whispered it. She didn't leave right after it happened. She went to the apartment, packed, and changed her dress, and about five or ten minutes later buzzed twice, like I had told her to. Tony had the car up there all that time, waiting for her, and he opened, pulled her in, and dropped her down to the basement. They went out by the alley, and when they came out on Twenty-third Street he got her a cab, and she left. That was the last he saw of her, and he didn't tell it to the police. While he was doing that, Harry was on the board in the lobby, and didn't pay much attention when he saw the fags going out, and neither did the guy from the Immigration Service.

How the cops found it out they didn't know, but they thought the fags must have bumped into one outside, or got scared and thought they better tell it anyway, or something. Tony said the cops were already in Winston's apartment before she left.

They went down and I went in the apartment again. With the phone cut off it was quiet enough now, but I began looking for the dictaphone. I couldn't find anything. I looked out the window to see if anybody was watching the building. There wasn't anybody out there. I began to think Sholto was imagining things.

Around two o'clock I got hungry and went out. The reporters were still down there, and almost mobbed me, but I jumped in a cab and told him to drive to Radio City. As soon as he got to Fourth Avenue I had him cut over to Second again, and come down, and got out at a restaurant around Twenty-third Street. I had something to eat and took down the number of the pay phone. When I got back to the apartment house, I whispered to the boy on the board if a Mr. Kugler called, to put him through. I went upstairs and called the restaurant phone. "Is Mr. Kugler there?"

"Hold the line, I'll see."

I held the line, and in a minute he was back. "No Mr. Kugler here now."

"When he comes in ask him to call Mr. Sharp. S-H-A-R-P."

"Yes sir, I'll tell him."

I hung up. In about twenty minutes the phone rang. "Mr. Sharp? This is Kugler."

"Oh, hello, Mr. Kugler. About those opera passes I promised you, I'm afraid I'll have to disappoint you for the time being. You may have read in the paper I'm having a little trouble now. Can you let me put that off till next week."

"Oh, all right, Mr. Sharp. Any time you say."

"Terribly sorry, Mr. Kugler."

I hung up. I knew then that Sholto knew what he was talking about. I didn't know any Mr. Kugler.

Harry kept bringing up new editions as they came out,

and the stuff that was coming in for me. They still hadn't got her. They found the taxi driver that rode her from Twenty-third Street. He said he took her down to Battery Park, she paid him with a five-dollar bill, so he had to go in the subway to get change, and then went off, carrying the valise. He told how Tony had flagged him, and Tony took another trip down to headquarters. It said the cops were considering the possibility she had jumped in the river, and that it might be dragged. The stuff that was coming in was a flock of telegrams, letters, and cards from every kind of nut you ever heard of, and opera fan, and shyster lawyer. But a couple of those wires weren't from nuts. One was from Panamier, saying the broadcast would temporarily be carried on by somebody else. And one was from Luther, saying no doubt I preferred not to have any more opera appearances until I got my affairs straightened out. The last afternoon edition had a story about Pudinsky. I felt my mouth go cold. He was the one person that might know about Winton and me. If he did he didn't say anything. He said what a fine guy Winston was, what a loyal friend, and defended him for calling up the Immigration people. He said Winston only had my best interests at heart.

I went out to eat around seven o'clock, dodged the reporters again, and had a steak in a place off Broadway. My picture was in every paper in town, but nobody seemed to notice me. One reason was, most of those pictures had been taken while I was in Hollywood, and I had put on a lot of weight since then. I wasn't exactly fat when I arrived from Mexico. Then I had a little trouble with my eyes, and had got glasses. I ate what I could, walked around a little, then around nine o'clock came back to the apartment. All the time I was walking I kept looking back, to see if I was followed. I tried not to, but I couldn't help it. In the cab, I kept twisting around, to see what was back of us.

There was another mountain of stuff when I came in, but I didn't bother to open it. I read back all the newspaper stuff again, and then there didn't seem to be anything to do but to go to bed. I lay there, first trying to think and then trying to sleep. I couldn't do either one. Then after a while I did drop off. I woke up in a cold sweat with moans coming out of my mouth. The whole day had been like some kind of a fever dream, chasing in and out of cabs, dodging reporters, trying to shake the police, if they were around, reading papers. Now for the first time I seemed to get it through my head the spot we were in. She was wanted for murder, and if they caught her they would burn her in the chair.

What waked me up the next morning was the phone. Harry was on the board. "I know you said not to call, Mr. Sharp, but there's a guy on the line, he kept calling all day yesterday, and now he's calling again, he says he's a friend of yours, and it's important, and he's got to talk to you, and I thought I better tell you."

"Who is he?"

"He won't say, but he said I should say the word Acapulco, something like that, to you, and you would know who it was."

"Put him through."

I hoped it might be Conners, and sure enough when I heard that "Is that you, lad?" I knew it was. He was pretty short. "I've been trying to reach you. I've called you, and wired you, and called again, and again—"

"I cut the phone calls off, and I haven't opened the last bunch of wires. You'd have been through in a second if they had told me. I want to see you, I've got to see you—"

"You have indeed. I have news."

"Stop! Don't say a word. I warn you that my phone is tapped, and everything you say is being heard."

"That occurred to me. That's why I refused to give my name. How can I get to you?"

"Wait a minute. Wait a minute. . . . Will you call me in five minutes? I'll have to figure a way—"

"In five minutes it is."

He hung up, and I tried to think of some way we could meet, and yet not tip off the cops over the phone where it would be. I couldn't think. He had said he had news,

158

and my head was just spinning around. Before I even had half an idea the phone rang again. "Well, lad, what's the word?"

"I haven't any. They're following me too, that's the trouble. Wait a minute, wait a minute—"

"I have something that might work."

"What is it?"

"Do you remember the time signature of the serenade you first sang to me?"

". . . Yes, of course."

"Write those figures down, the two of them, one beside the other. Now write them again, the same way. You should have a number of four figures."

I jumped up, got a pen, and wrote the numbers on the memo pad. It was the Don Giovanni serenade, and time signature is 6/8. I wrote 6868. . . . "All right, I've got it."

"Now subtract from it this number." He gave me a number to subtract. I did it. "That is the number of the pay telephone I'm at. The exchange number is Circle 6. Go out to another pay telephone and call me there."

"In twenty minutes. As soon as I get dressed."

I jumped into my clothes, ran up to a drugstore, and called. Whether they were around the booth, listening to me, I didn't care. They couldn't hear what was coming in at the other end. "Is that you, lad?"

"Yes. What news?"

"I have her. She's going down the line with me. I'm at the foot of Seventeenth Street, and I slip my hawsers at midnight tonight. If you wish to see her before we leave, come aboard some time after eleven, but take care you're not detected."

"How did you find her?"

"I didn't. She found me. She's been aboard since yesterday, if you had answered your phone."

"I'll be there. I'll thank you then."

I went back to the apartment, cut out the fooling around, and began to think. I checked over every last thing I had to do that day, then made a little program in my mind of what I was to do first, and what I was to do after that. I

159

knew I would be tailed, and I planned it all on that basis. The first thing I did was to go up to Grand Central, and look up trains for Rye. I found there was a local leaving around ten that night. I came out of there, went in a store and bought some needles and thread. Then I went down to the bank. I still had over six thousand dollars in hundred-dollar bills, but I needed more than that. I drew out ten thousand, half of it in thousand-dollar bills, twenty-five hundred more in hundreds, and the rest in fives and tens, with about fifty ones I stuffed all that in my pockets, and went home with it. I remembered about the two shirts I had worn out of the hotel in Mexico, and pulled one just like it. I took two pairs of drawers, put one pair inside the other, sewed the bottoms of each leg together, then quilted that money in, all except the ones, and some fives and tens, that I put in my pockets. I put the drawers on. They felt a little heavy, but I could get my trousers over them without anything showing. Tony came up. They had got out of him how he had called the taxi, and he was almost crying because he had squealed. I told him it didn't make any difference.

When dinner time came, instead of going out I had something sent in. Then I packed. I shoved a stack of newspapers and heavy stuff into a traveling case, and locked it. When I dressed I put on a pair of gray flannel pants I had left over from Hollywood, and over my shirt a dark red sweater. I put on a coat, and over that a light topcoat. I picked out a gray hat, shoved it on the side of my head. I looked at myself in the mirror and I looked like what I wanted to look like, a guy dressed up to take a trip. After drawing the money, I knew they would expect that. That was why I had planned it the way I had.

At nine thirty, I called Tony, had him take my bag down and call a cab, shook hands with him, and called out to the driver, "Grand Central." We turned into Second Avenue. Two cars started up, down near Twenty-first Street, and one left the curb just behind us as we turned west on Twenty-third. When we turned into Fourth, they turned too. When we got to Grand Central they were still with us, and five guys got out, none of them looking at me. I gave my bag to a redcap, went to the ticket office, bought a ticket for Rye, then went out to the news-stand and bought a paper. When I mixed with the crowd at the head of the ramp I started to read it. Three of the five were there too, all of them reading papers.

The redcap put me aboard, but I didn't let him pick the car. I did that myself. It was a local, all day-coaches, but I wanted one without vestibule. It happened to be the smoker, so that looked all right. I took a seat near the door and went on reading my paper. The three took seats further up, but one of them reversed his seat and sat so he could see me. I didn't even look up as we pulled out, didn't look up as we pulled into a Hundred and Twenty-fifth Street, didn't look up as we pulled out. But when the train had slid about twenty feet, I jumped up, left my bag where it was, walked three steps to the car platform, and skipped off. I never stopped. I zipped right out to a taxi, jumped in, told him to drive to Grand Central, and to step on it. He started up. I kept my eyes open. Nobody was behind us, that I could see.

When he turned into upper Park, I tapped on the glass and said I was too late for my train, that he should go to Eighth Avenue and Twenty-third Street. He nodded and kept on. I took off the hat, the topcoat, and the coat and laid them in a little pile on the seat. When we got to Eighth and Twenty-third I got out, took out a five-dollar bill. "I left some stuff in the car, two coats and a hat. Take them up to Grand Central and check them to leave them. Leave the three checks at the information desk, in my name, Mr. Henderson. There's no hurry. Any time to-night will do."

"Yes sir, yes sir."

He grabbed the five, touched his hat, and went off. I started down Eighth Avenue. Instead of a guy all dressed up to go away, I was just a guy without a hat, walking down for a stroll on a spring night. I looked at my watch. It was a quarter to eleven. I back-tracked up to Twenty-third Street and went into a movie.

At twenty after, I came out, started down Eighth Avenue again, and walked to Seventeenth Street. I took my time, looked in windows, keep peeping at my watch. When I cut over to the pier it was a quarter to twelve. I followed the signs to the *Port of Cobh*, strolled aboard. Nobody stopped me. Up at the winch I saw something that looked familiar. I went up and put my arm around him.

"She's back in your old cabin—and you're late."

I went back there, knocked, and stepped in. It was dark in there, but a pair of arms were around me before I even got the door shut, and a pair of lips were against mine, and I tried to say something, and couldn't and she tried to say something and couldn't and we just sat on one of the berths, and held on to each other.

In almost no time there was a knock on the door and he stepped in. "You'll be going ashore now. Why didn't you get here sooner?"

"What are you talking about?"

"I cast my hawsers in two minutes."

"Hawsers, hell. I'm going with her."

"No, Hoaney. Goodbye, goodbye, now you are free, remember, Juana, but come not. No, I have much money now, I be all right. Now, kiss, I love you much."

"I'm going with you."

"No, no!"

"Lad, you don't know what you're saying. Alone, she can vanish like the mist. With you, she's doomed."

"I'm going with her."

He went out. A bell sounded on the tugboat, and we began to move. We looked out. When we straightened out in the river we were looking at the Jersey side. We slipped past it, and pretty soon we stepped out and found him on the bridge. He was at the far end of it, looking out at the Long Island side. I said something, but he paid no attention, and pointed. A cluster of lights was bearing down on us. "It's a police boat, and she's headed right for us."

We stood watching it, hardly daring to breathe. It came on, then cut across our bows toward Staten Island. We picked up speed. The first swell lifted our nose. She put her hand in mine, and gave it a little squeeze.

13

WE WERE IN GUATEMALA, though, before we really knew what we were up against, or I did. The trip down was just one nightmare of biting our fingernails and listening to every news broadcast we could pick up, to see if they were on our trail yet. In between, I stuffed myself with food and beer, to put on more weight, and let my moustache grow, and plucked my eyebrows to give my face a different expression, and stood around in the sun, to tan. All I thought about was that radio, and what it was going to tell us. Then at Havana I was running around like a wild man, still trying to beat them to the punch. I found a tailor shop, and put in a rush order for clothes, and then at a little bootleg printshop I got myself a lot of fake papers fixed up, all in the name of Guiseppe Di Nola and where she figured in them, Lola Deminguez Di Nola. I speak Italian like a Neapolitan, and changed myself into an Italian as fast as the tailor, the printer, the barber, and all the rest of them could work on me. As well as I could tell, I got by all right, and none of them had any idea who I was. But one thing kept gnawing at me, and that was the hello I had said to Conners on that first broadcast. Sooner or later, I knew, somebody was going to remember it and check back, and then we would be sunk. I wanted to get a thousand miles away from that ship, and any place she would touch on her way down to Rio.

I had to work fast, because all we had was a three-day layover. As soon as my first suit was ready, I put my fake papers in a briefcase and went over to Pan-American. I found all we would really need was a vaccination certificate for each of us. The rest was a matter of tourist papers that they furnished. I told them to make out the ticket and that I would have the certificates at the airport in the morning. I went over to American Express and bought travelers' checks, then went down to the boat and got her. I had her put on some New York clothes, and we went ashore. Then we went to a little hotel off the Prado. Conners wasn't there when we left, and I had to scribble a note to him, and call that a goodbye. It seemed a terrible thing to beat it without even shaking his hand, but I was afraid even to leave our hotel address with anyone on board, for fear some U.S. detective would show up and they would tip him off. So far, none of them on the ship knew us. He had run into a strike at Seattle in the winter, and cleared with an entirely new crew, even officers. He had carried us as Mr. and Mrs. Di Nola, and Mr. and Mrs. Di Nola just disappeared.

There was no hotel doctor, but they knew of one, and got him around, and he vaccinated us, and gave us our certificates. About six o'clock I went around to the tailor and got the rest of my suits. They were all right, and so were the shoes, shirts, and the rest of the stuff I had bought. The tropicals were double-breasted, with a kind of a Monte Carlo look, the pin-stripe had white piping on the vest and the gray had black velvet, the hats were fedoras, one green, the other black, with a Panama thrown in to go with the tropicals. The shoes were two-toned. On appearance, I was as Italian as Mussolini, and I was surprised to see I looked quite a lot like him. I got out my razor and gave the moustache an up-cut under each corner. That helped. It was two weeks out now, and plenty black, with some gray in it. Those gray hairs startled me. I hadn't known they were there.

In the morning we went to the airport, showed the certificates, and were passed through. The way the trip broke, we could make better time by going through to Vera Cruz, and then turning south, than by making the change at Mérida. There had been some switch on planes, and that would save us a day. I didn't want to spend one more hour in Mexico than I had to, so I said that suited me. Where we were going I had no idea, except that we were going a long way from Havana, but where we were booked for was Guatemala. That seemed to be a kind of a terminus, and to go on from there we would have to have more papers than they could furnish us with at Havana. She got sick as a dog as soon as we took off, and I, and the steward, and the pilots thought it was airsickness. But when it still kept up, after we got to the hotel in Vera Cruz, I knew it was the vaccination. She was all right, though, the next day, and kept looking down at the country we were going over. We had the Gulf of Mexico under us for a little while after we hauled out of Vera Cruz, and then as we were working down toward Tapachula we were over the Pacific. She had to have all that explained to her. She had never got the oceans quite straight, and how we could leave one, and then pick up another almost before we had time to look at the pictures in the magazines, had to be blue-printed for her, with drawings. To her, I think all countries were square, like a bean patch with lines of maguey around it, and it was hard for her to get through her head how any country, and especially Mexico, could be wide at the top and narrow at the bottom.

At Guatemala, we marched from the plane into the pavilion with a loud speaker blaring the Merry Widow waltz, a barefoot Indian girl gave us coffee, and then after a while an American in a flyer's uniform came and explained to me, in some kind of broken Italian, what I would have to do to go on down the line, if that was what I expected to do. I thanked him, we got our luggage, and went to the Palace Hotel. Then I got to thinking:

Why are we going down the line? Why is Chile any better than Guatemala? Our big danger comes every time we fool with papers, and if we're all right so far, why not let well enough alone, and dig in? We couldn't stay on at the hotel, because it was full of Americans, Germans, English and all kinds of people, and sooner or later one of them would know me. But we might rent a place. I sent her down to the desk to ask how we went about it, and when we found out we didn't have to sign any police forms, we went out and got a house. It was a furnished house, just around the block from the hotel, and the gloomiest dump I ever laid eyes on, with walnut chairs, and horse-hair sofas, and sea shells, and coconut shells carved into skulls, and everything else you could think of. But there was a bathroom in it, and it didn't look like we would find one any better. The lady that owned it was Mrs. Gonzalez, and she wanted it understood that she didn't really have to rent the house, that she came of an old coffee family, that she preferred to live out of town, at the lake, on account of her health. We said we understood that perfectly, and closed at a hundred and fifty quetzals a month. A quetzal exchanges even with a dollar.

So in a couple of days we moved in. I found a Japanese couple that didn't speak any English, Italian, or Spanish, and we had to wigwag, but there was no chance of their finding out too much. I was practicing Spanish morning, noon and night, so she and I would be able to talk in front of other people without using English, and I tried to speak it with an Italian accent, but I still wasn't sure I was getting away with it. With the Japs, though, it was safe around the house.

So then we breathed a little easier, and began to shake down into a routine. Daytime we'd lay around, mostly upstairs, in our bedroom. At night we'd walk down to the park and listen to the band. But we'd always sit well away from it, on a lonely bench. Then we'd come back, flit the mosquitoes, and go to bed. There was nothing else to do, even if we had thought it was safe to do it. Guatemala is the Japan of Central America. They've copied everything. They've got Mexican music, American movies, Scotch whisky, German delicatessens, Roman religion, and everything else imported you can think of. But they forgot to put anything of their own in, and what comes out is a place you could hardly tell from Glendale, California, on a bet. It's clean, modern, prosperous, and dull. And the weather gives you plenty of chance to find out how dull it really is. We hit there in June, at the height of the rainy season. It's not supposed to rain in Central America, by the books, but that's wrong. It rains plenty, a cold, gray rain that sometimes keeps up for two days at a time. Then when the sun comes out it's so sticky hot you can hardly breathe, and the mosquitos start up. The air gets you down almost as bad as it does in Mexico. Guatemala City is nearly a mile up in the air, and at night that feeling of suffocation comes over you, so you think you'll die if you don't get something in your lungs you can breathe.

Little by little, a change came over her. Mind you, from the time we left New York we hadn't said one word about Winston, or what she did, or whether it was right or wrong, or anything about it. That was done, and we steered around it. We talked about the Japs, the mosquitoes, where Conners was by now, things like that, and so long as we jumped at every noise, we seemed to be nearer than we ever had been. But after that eased off, and we began to kid ourselves we were safe, she began moping to herself, and now and then I'd catch her looking at me. Then I noticed that another thing we never talked about was my singing. And then one night, just as we started downstairs to go out in the park, just mechanically I did a little turn, and in another second would have cut loose a high one. I saw this look of horror on her face, and choked it off. She listened, to see if the Japs had caught it. They seemed to be in the kitchen, so we went down. Then it came to me, the spot I was in. On the way down I hadn't even thought about singing. But here, and any other place south of the Rio Grande, for that matter, my voice was just as familiar as bananas. My picture, in the lumberjack suit, was still plastered all over the Panamier show windows, Pablo Buñan had played the town not a month before, even the kids were whistling My Pal Babe. Unless I was going to send her to the chair, I couldn't ever sing again.

I tried not to think about it, and so long as I could read, or do something to get my mind off it, I wouldn't. But you can't read all the time, and in the afternoon I'd get to wishing she'd wake up from her siesta, so we could talk, or practice Spanish, and I could shake it off. Then I began to get this ache across the bridge of my nose. You see, it wasn't that I was thinking about the fine music I couldn't sing any more, or the muted song that was lost to the world, or anything like that. It was simpler than that, and worse. A voice is a physical thing, and if you've got one, it's like any other physical thing. It's in you, and it's got to come out. The only thing I can compare it with is when you haven't been with a woman for a long time, and and you get so you think if you don't find one soon, you'll go insane. The bridge of the nose is where your voice focuses, where you get that little pull when you cut loose, and that was where I began to feel it. I'd talk, and read, and eat, and try to forget it, and it would go away, but then it would come back.

Then I began to have these dreams. I'd be up there, and they'd be playing my cue, and it would be time for me to come in, and I'd open my mouth, and nothing would come out of it. I'd be dying to sing, and couldn't. A murmur would go over the house, he'd rap the orchestra to attention, look at me, and start the cue again. Then I'd wake up. Then one night, just after she had gone over to her bed, something happened so we did talk about it. In Central America, they've got radios all over the place, and there were three in the block back of us, and one of them had been setting me nuts all day. It was getting London, and they don't have any of that advertising hooey over there. The whole Barber of Seville had come over in the afternoon, with only a couple of small cuts, and at night they had played the Third, Fifth, and Seventh Beethoven symphonies. Then, around ten o'clock, a guy began to sing the serenade from Don Giovanni, the same thing I had sung for Conners at Acapulco, the same thing I had sung the night I came in big at the Metropolitan. He was pretty good. Then, at the end, he did the same *messa di voce* that I had done. I kind of laughed, in the dark. ". . . Well, he's heard me sing it."

She didn't say anything, and then I felt she was crying. I went over there. "What's the matter?"

"Hoaney, Hoaney, you leave me now. You go. We say goodbye."

168

"Well—what's the big idea?"

"You no know who that was? Who sing? Just now?"

"No. Why?"

"That was you."

She turned away from me then, and began to shake from her sobs, and I knew I had been listening to one of my own phonograph records, put on the air after the main program was over. ". . . Well? What of it?"

But I must have sounded a little sick. She got up, snapped on the light, and began walking around the room. She was stark naked, the way she generally slept on hot nights, but she was no sculptor's model now. She looked like an old woman, with her shoulders slumped down, her feet sliding along in a flat-footed Indian walk, her eyes set dead ahead, like two marbles, and her hair hanging straight over her face. When the sobs died off a little, she pulled out a bureau drawer, got out a gray *rebozo*, and pulled that over her shoulders. Then she started shuffling around again. If she had had a donkey beside her, it would have been any hag, from Mexicali to Tapachula. Then she began to talk. ". . . So. Now you go? Now we say *adiós*."

"What the hell are you talking about? You think I'm going to walk out on you now?"

"I kill these man, yes. For what he do to you, for what he do to me, I have to kill him. I know these thing at once, that night, when I hear of the *inmigración*, that I have to kill him. I ask you? No. Then what I do? Yes. What I do!"

"Listen, for Christ's sake—"

"What I do? You tell me, what I do?"

"Goddam if I know. Laughed at him, for one thing."

"I say goodbye. Yes, I come to you, say remember Juana, kiss you one time, *adiós*. Yes, I kill him, but then is goodbye. I know. I say so. You remember?"

"I don't know. Will you cut it out, and—"

"Then you come to boat. I am weak. I love you much. But what I do then? What I say?"

"Goodbye, I suppose. Is that all you know to say?"

"Yes. Once more I say goodbye. The *capitán*, he know too, he tell you go. You no go. You come. Once more, I love you much, I am glad. . . . Now, once more. Three times, I tell you go. It is the end. I tell you, *goodbye.*"

She didn't look at me. She was shooting it at me with her eyes staring straight again, and her feet carrying her back and forth with that sliding, shuffling walk. I opened my mouth two or three times to stall some more, but couldn't, looking at her. "Well, what are you going to do? Will you tell me that? Do you know?"

"Yes. You go. You give me money, not much, but little bit. Then I work, get little job, maybe kitchen *muchacha*, nobody know me, look like all other *muchacha*, I get job, easy. Then I go to priest, confess my *pecado*—"

"That's what I've been waiting for. I knew that was coming. Now let me tell you something. You confess that *pecado*, and right there is where you lose."

"I no lose. I give money to church, they no turn me in. Then I have peace. Then some time I go back to Mexico."

"And what about me?"

"You go. You sing. You sing for radio. I hear. I remember. You remember. Maybe. Remember little dumb *muchacha*—"

"Listen, little dumb *muchacha*, that's all swell, except for one thing. When we hooked up, we hooked up for good, and—"

"Why you talk so? It is the end! Can you no see these thing? It is the end! You no go, what then? They take me back. Me only, they never find. You, yes. They take me back, and what they do to me? In Mexico, maybe nothing, unless he was *político*. In New York, I know, you know. The *soldados* come, they put the *pañuelo* over the eyes, they take me to wall, they shoot. Why you do these things to me? You love me, yes. *But it is the end!*"

I tried to argue, got up and tried to catch her, to make her quit that walking around. She slipped away from me. Then she flung herself down on her bed and lay there staring up at the ceiling. When I came to her she waved me away. From that time on she slept in her bed and I slept in mine, and nothing I could do would break her down.

I didn't leave her, I couldn't leave her. It wasn't only that I was insane about her. What was between us had completely reversed since we started out. In the beginning, I thought of her like she had said, as a little dumb *muchacha* that I was nuts about, that I loved to touch and sleep with and play with. But now I had found out that in all the main things of my life she was stronger than I was, and I had got so I had to be with her. It wouldn't have done any good to leave her. I'd have been back as fast as a plane could carry me.

For a week after that, we'd lie there in the afternoon, saying nothing, and then she began putting on her clothes and going out. I'd lie there, trying not to think about singing, praying for strength not to suck in a bellyful and cut it loose. Then it popped in my mind about the priests, and I got in a cold sweat that that was where she was going. So one day I followed her. But she went past the Cathedral, and then I got ashamed of myself and turned around and came back.

I had to do something with myself, though, so when she went I began going to the baseball games. From that you can imagine how much there was to do in Guatemala, that I would go to the baseball game. They've got some kind of a league between Managua, Guatemala, San Salvador, and some other Central American towns, and they get as excited about it as they get in Chicago over a World Series, and yell at the ump, and all the rest of it. Busses run out there, but I walked. The fewer people that got a close look at me, the better I liked it. One day I found myself watching the pitcher on the San Salvador team. The papers gave his name as Barrios, but he must have been an American, or anyway have lived in the United States, from his motion. Most of those Indians handle a ball jerky, and fight it so they make more errors than you could believe. But this guy had the old Lefty Gomez motion, loose, easy, so his whole weight went in the pitch, and more smoke than all the rest of them had put together. I sat looking at him, taking in those motions, and then all of a sudden I felt my heart stop. Was it coming out in me again, this thing that had got me when I met Winston? Was that kid out there really doing things to me that had nothing to do with baseball? Was it having its effect, her putting me out of her bed?

I got up and left. I know now it was just nerves, that when Winston died that chapter ended. But I didn't then. I tried to put it out of my mind, and couldn't. I didn't go to the ball games any more, but then, after a couple of weeks, I got to thinking: Am I going to turn into the priest again? Am I going to give up everything else in this Christ-forsaken dump, and then lose my voice too? It began to be an obsession with me that I had to have a woman, that if I didn't have a woman I was sunk.

She didn't go with me to hear the band play any more. She stayed home and went to bed. One night, when I went out, instead of heading for the park, I flagged a taxi. "La Locha."

"Sí, Señor, La Locha."

I had heard guys at the ball game talking about La Locha's, but I didn't know where it was. It turned out to be on Tenth Avenue, but the district was on a different system from in Mexico. There were regular houses, with red lights over the door, all according to Hoyle. I rang, and an Indian let me in. A whorehouse, I guess, is the same all over the world. There was a big room, with a phonograph on one side, a radio on the other, and an electric piano in the middle, with a stained-glass picture of Niagara Falls in the front, that lit up whenever somebody put in a nickel. The wallpaper had red roses all over it, and at one end was a bar. Back of the bar was an oil painting of a nude, and in the cabinet under it were stacks and stacks of long square cans. When a guy in Guatemala really wants to show the girls a good time, he blows them to canned asparagus.

The Indian looked at me pretty funny, and after he went back, so did the woman at the bar. I thought at first it was the Italian way I was speaking Spanish, but then it seemed to be something about my hat. An Army officer was at a little table, reading a newspaper. He had his hat on, and then I remembered and put mine on. I ordered

172

cerveza, and three girls came in. They stood on the rail and began loving me up. Two of them were Indian, but one of them was white, and she looked the cleanest. I put my arm around her, and after the other two got their drinks, they went over with the officer. One of them turned on the radio, and the other one and the officer began to dance. My girl and I danced. By rights I guess she was fairly pretty. She couldn't have been more than twenty-one or two, and even in the sweater and green dress she had on, you could see she had a pretty good shape. But she kept playing with my hand, and everything I'd say to her, she'd answer in a little high squeak of a voice that got on my nerves. I asked her what her name was. She said María.

We had another dance, but God knows there was no point in keeping that up. I asked her if she wanted to go upstairs, and she was leading me out the door even before the tune was over.

We went up, she took me in a room, and snapped on the light. It was just the same old whore's bedroom, except for one thing. On the bureau was a signed photograph of Enzo Luchetti, an old bass I had sung with years before, in Florence. My heart skipped a beat. If he was in town, that meant I have to get out, and get out fast. I picked it up and asked her who it was. She said she didn't know. Another girl had had the room before she came, a fine girl that had been in Europe, but she had got enferma and had to leave. I put it down and said it looked like an Italian. She asked if I wasn't Italian. I said yes.

There didn't seem to be much to do, then, but get at it. She began dropping off her clothes. I began dropping off mine. She snapped off the light and we lay down on the bed. I didn't want her, and yet I was excited, in some kind of a queer, unnatural way, because I knew I had to have her. It didn't seem possible that anything could be over so quick and amount to so little. We lay there, and I tried to talk to her, but there wasn't anything to talk to. Then we had another, and next thing I knew I was dressing. Ten quetzals. I gave her fifteen. She got awfully friendly then, but it was like having a poodle bitch trying to jump in your lap. It was only a little after ten when I got home, but Juana was asleep. I undressed in the dark, got into bed, and thought I would get some peace. Next thing, the conductor threw the stick on me, and I tried to sing, and the chorus stood around looking at me, and I began yelling, trying to tell them why I couldn't. When I woke up, those yells were still echoing in my ears, and she was standing over me, shaking me.

"Hoaney! What is it?"

"Just a dream."

"So."

She went back to bed. Not only the bridge of my nose, but the whole front of my face was aching so it was two hours before I dropped off again.

From then on I was like somebody threshing around in a fever, and the more I threshed the worse the fever got. I went around there every night, and when I was so sick of María I couldn't even look at her any more, I tried the Indian girls, and when I got sick of them I went in other places, and tried other Indian girls. Then I began picking girls off the street, and in cafés, and taking them in to cheap hotels off the park. They didn't ask me to register and I didn't volunteer. I paid the money, took them in, and around eleven o'clock left them there and went home. Then I went back to La Locha's and started up with María again. The more I had of them the worse I wanted to sing. And all that time there was only one woman in the world that I really wanted, and that was Juana. But Juana had turned to ice. After that one little flash, when I woke her up with my nightmare, she went back to treating me like she just barely knew me. We spoke, talked about whatever had to be talked about, but whenever I tried to push it further than that, she didn't even hear me.

One night the Pagliacci cue began to play, and I was just about to step through the curtain and face that conductor again. But I was almost used to it by now, and woke up. I was about to drop off again, when a horrible realization came to me. I wasn't home. I was in bed with María. I had been lying there listening to her squeak about how the rains would be over soon, and then the

174

good weather would come, and must have gone to sleep. I was the star customer there by now, and she must have turned off the light and just let me alone. I jumped up, snapped on the light, and looked at my watch. It was two o'clock. I jumped into my clothes, left a twenty-quetzal note on the bureau, and ran downstairs. Things were just getting good down in the main room. The army, the judiciary, the coffee kingdom, and the banana empire were all on hand, the girls were stewed, the asparagus was going down in bunches, and the radio, the phonograph, and the electric piano were all going at once. I never stopped. A whole row of taxis were parked up and down the street outside. I jumped in one, went home. A light was on upstairs. I let myself in and started up there.

Halfway up, I felt something coming at me. I fell back a step and braced myself for her to hit me. She didn't. She shot by me on the stairs, and in the half light I saw she was dressed to go out. She had on red hat, red dress, and red shoes, with gold stockings, and rouge smeared all over her face, but I didn't catch all that until later. All I saw was that she was got up like some kind of hussy, and I took about six steps at one jump and caught her at the door. She didn't scream. She never screamed, or talked loud, or anything like that. She sank her teeth into my hand and grabbed for the door again. I caught her once more, and we fought like a couple of animals. Then I threw her against the door, got my arms around her from behind, and carried her upstairs, with her heels cutting dents in my shins. When we got in the bedroom I turned her loose, and we faced each other panting, her eyes like two points of light, my hands slippery with blood. "What's the rush? Where you going?"

"Where you think? To the Locha, where you come from."

That was one between the eyes. I didn't know she had even heard of La Locha's. But I dead-panned as well as I could.

"What's the locha? I don't seem to place it."

"So, once more you lie."

"I don't even know what you're talking about. I went for a walk and got lost, that's all."

"You lie, now another time you lie. You think these girl no tell me about crazy Italian who come every night? You think they no tell me?"

"So that's where you spend your afternoons."

"Yes."

She stood smiling at me, letting it soak in. I kept thinking I ought to kill her, that if I was a man I'd take her by the throat and choke her till her face turned black. But I didn't want to kill her. I just felt shaky in the knees, and weak, and sick. "Yes, that is where I go, I find little *muchacha* for company, little *muchacha* like me, for nice little talk and cup of chocolate after siesta. And what these little *muchacha* talk? Only about crazy Italian, who come every night, give five-quetzal tip." She pitched her voice into Maria's squeak. "*Sí. Cinco quetzales.*"

I was licked. When I had run my tongue around my lips enough that they stopped fluttering, I backed down. "All right. Once more I'll cut out the lying. Yes, I was there. Now will you stop this show, so we can talk?"

She looked away, and I saw her lips begin to twitch. I went in the bathroom, and started to wash the blood off my hand. I wanted her to follow me in, and I knew if she did, she'd break. She didn't. "No! No more talk! You no go, then I go! *Adiós!*"

She was down, and out the front door, before I even got to the head of the stairs.

14

I RAN OUT ON THE STREET just as a taxi pulled away from the corner. I yelled, but it didn't stop. There was no other taxi in sight, and I didn't find one till I went clear around the block to the stand in front of the hotel. I had him take me back to La Locha's. By that time there were at least twenty cabs parked up and down the street, and things were going strong in all the houses. It kept riding me that even if she had gone in the place, they might lie to me about it, and I couldn't be sure unless I searched the joint, and that meant they would call the cops. I went to the first cab that was parked there and asked him if a girl in a red dress had gone in any of the houses. He said no. I gave him a quetzal and said if she showed, he was to come in La Locha's and let me know. I went to the next driver, and the next, and did the same. By the time I had handed out quetzals to half a dozen of them, I knew that ten seconds after she got out of her cab I would know it. I went back to La Locha's. No girl in a red dress had come, said the Indian. I set up drinks for all hands, sat down with one of the girls, and waited.

Around three o'clock the judiciary began to leave, and after them the army, and then all the others that weren't spending the night. At four o'clock they put me out. Two or three of my taxi drivers were still standing there, and they swore that no girl in a red dress, or any other kind of dress, had come to any house in the street all night. I passed out a couple more quetzals, had one of them drive me home. She wasn't there. I routed out the Japs. It was an hour's job of pidgin Spanish and wig-wagging to find out what they knew, but after a while I got it straight. Around nine o'clock she had started to pack. Then she got a cab, put her things in it, and went out. Then she came back, and when she found out I wasn't home, went out. When she came back the second time, around midnight, she had on the red dress, and kept walking around upstairs waiting for me. Then I came home, and there was the commotion, and she went out again, and hadn't been back since.

I shaved, cleaned the dried blood off my hand, changed my clothes. Around eight o'clock I tried to eat some breakfast and couldn't. Around nine o'clock the bell rang. A taxi driver was at the door. He said some of his friends had told him I was looking for a lady in a red dress. He said he had driven her, and could take me to where he left her. I took my hat, got in, and he drove me around to a cheap hotel, one of those I had been to myself. They said yes, a lady of that description had been there. She had come earlier in the evening, changed her clothes once and gone out, then came back late and left an early call. She hadn't registered. About seven thirty this morning she had gone out. I asked how she was dressed. They just shrugged. I asked if she had taken a cab. They said they didn't know. I rode back to the house, and tried to piece it together. One thing began to stick out of it now. My being out late, that wasn't why she had left. She was leaving anyway, and after she had moved out she had come back, probably to say goodbye. Then when she found I wasn't there she had got sore, gone to the hotel again, changed into the red dress, and come back to harpoon me with how she was going back to her old life. Whether she had gone back to it, or what she had done, I had no more idea than the man in the moon.

I waited all that day, and the next. I was afraid to go to the police. I could have checked on the Tenth Avenue end of it in a minute. They keep a card for every girl on the street, with her record and picture, and if she had gone there, she would have had to report. But once I set them on her trail, that might be the beginning of the end. And I didn't even know what name she was using. So far, even with the drivers and at the hotel, I hadn't given her name or mine. I had spoken of her as the girl in the red dress, but even that wouldn't do any more. If they couldn't remember how she was dressed when she left the hotel, it was a cinch she wasn't wearing red. I lay around, and waited, and cursed myself for giving her five thousand quetzals cash, just in case. With that, she could hide out on me for a year. And then it dawned on me for the first time that with that she could go anywhere she pleased. She could have left town.

I went right over to one of the open-front drugstores, went in a booth, and called Pan-American. I spoke English. I said I was an American, that I had met a Mexican lady at the hotel and promised to give her some pictures I had taken of her, but I hadn't seen her for a couple of days and I was wondering if she had left town. They asked me her name. I said I didn't know her name, but they might identify her by a fur coat she was probably carrying. They asked me to hold the line. Then they said yes, the porter remembered a fur coat he had handled for a Mexican lady, that if I'd hold the line they'd see if they could get me her name and address. I held the line again. Then they said they were sorry, they didn't have her address, but her name was Mrs. Di Nola, and she had left on the early plane the day before for Mexico City.

Mexico looked exactly the same, the burros, the goats, the *pulquerías*, the markets, but I didn't have time for any of that. I went straight from the airport to the Majestic, a new hotel that had opened since I left there, registered as Di Nola, and started to look for her. I didn't go to the police, I didn't make any inquiries, and I didn't do any walking, for fear I'd be recognized. I just put a car under charter, had the driver go around and around, and took a chance that sooner or later I'd see her. I went up and down the Guauhtemolzin until the girls would jeer at us every time we showed up, and the driver had to wave and say "*postales*," to shut them up. Buying postcards seemed to be the stock alibi if you were just rubbering around. I went up and down every avenue, where the crowds were thickest, and the more the traffic held us up, the better it suited me. I kept my eyes glued to the sidewalk. At night, we drove past every café, and around eleven o'clock, when the picture theatres closed, we drove past them, on the chance I'd see her coming out. I didn't tell him what I wanted, I just told him where to drive.

By the end of that day I hadn't even caught a glimpse of her. I told the driver to be on deck promptly at eleven the next morning, which was Sunday. We started out, and I had him drive me into Chapultepec Park, and I was sure I'd see her there. The whole city turns out there every Sunday morning to listen to the band, ride horses, wink at the girls, and just walk. We rode around for three hours, past the zoo, the bandstand, the boats in the lake, the chief of the mounted police and his daughter, so many times we got dizzy, and still no trace of her. In the afternoon we kept it up, driving all over the city going every place there might be a crowd. There was no bull-fight. The season for them hadn't started, but we combed the boulevards, the suburbs, and every place else I could think of. He asked if I'd need him after supper. I said no, to report at ten in the morning. It wasn't getting me any-where, and I wanted to think what I was going to do next. After dinner I took a walk, to try and figure out something, I passed two or three people I had known, but they never gave me a tumble. What left Mexico was a big, hard, and starved-looking American. What came back was a middle-aged wop, with a pot on him so big it hid his feet. When I got to the Palacio de Bellas Artes, it was all lit up. I crossed toward it, and thought I'd sit on a stone bench and keep an eye on the crowd that was com-ing in. But when I got near enough to read the signs I saw it was Rigoletto they were giving and this dizzy, drunken feeling swept over me, that I should go in there and sing it, and take the curse off the flop, and show them how I could do it. I cut back, and turned the cor-ner into the town.

Next to the bullring box office is a café. I went in there, ordered an apricot brandy, and sat down. I told myself to forget about the singing, that what I was trying to do was find her. The place was pretty full, and three of four guys were standing in front of one of the booth tables against the wall. Through them I caught a flash of red, and my mouth went dry. They went back to their own table and I was looking right at her.

She was with Triesca, the bullfighter, and more guys kept coming up to him, shaking his hand, and going away again. She saw me, and looked away quick. Then he saw me. He kept looking at me, and then he placed me. He said something to her, and laughed. She nodded, kept looking off somewhere with a strained face, and then half laughed. Then he ogled at me. By the way both of them were acting I knew he didn't connect me with New York, and maybe he didn't know anything about the New York stuff at all. All he saw was a guy that had once taken his girl away from him, and had then turned out to be a fag. But that was enough for him. He began putting on an act that the whole room was roaring at in a minute. Her face got hard and set. I felt the blood begin to pound in my head.

A mariachi came in. He threw them a couple of pesos, and they screeched three or four times. Then he got a real idea. He called the leader, and whispered, and they started *Cielito Lindo*. But instead of them singing it, he got up and sang it. He sang right at me, in a high, simpering falsetto, with gestures. They laughed like hell. If she had dead-panned, I think I would have sat there and taken it. But she didn't. She laughed. I don't know why. Maybe she was just nervous. Maybe she played it the way the rest of them expected her to play it. Maybe she was still sore about Guatemala. Maybe she really thought it was funny, that I should be following her around like some puppy after she had hooked up with another man. I don't know, and I didn't think about any of that at the time. When I saw that laugh, I got a dizzy, wanton feeling in my head, and I knew that all hell couldn't stop me from what I was going to do.

He got to the end of the verse, and they gave him a laugh and a big hand. He struck a pose for the chorus, and then I laughed too, and stood up. That suprised him, and he hesitated. And then I shot it:

> Ay, Ay, Ay, Ay!
> Canta y no llores
> Porque cantando se alegran
> Cielito lindo
> Los corazones!

It was like gold, bigger than it had ever been, and when I finished I was panting from the excitement of it. He stood there, looking thick, and then came this roar of applause. The mariachi leader began jabbering at me, and they started it again. I sang it through, drunk from the way it felt, drunk from the look on her face. On the second chorus, I sang it right at her, soft and slow. But at the end I put in a high one, closed my eyes and swelled it, held it till the glasses rattled, and then came off it.

When I opened my eyes wide she wasn't looking at me.

She was looking past the bar, behind me. The mob was cheering, people were crowding in from the street, and all over the place they were passing it around, *"El Panamier Trovador!"* But in a booth was an officer, yelling into a telephone. How long that kept up I don't know. They were all around me, jabbering things for me to sing. Next thing I knew, she was running for the door, Triesca after her. But I was ahead of him. I rammed through the crowd, and when I got to the street I could see the red of her dress, half a block away. I started to run. I hadn't gone two steps before some cops grabbed me. I wrestled with them. From up the street came shots, and people began to run and scream. Then from somewhere came a rattle of Spanish, and I heard the word "gringo." They turned me loose, and I ran on. Ahead of me were more cops, and people standing around. I saw something red on the pavement. When I pushed through she was lying there, and beside her, this quivering smile on his face, was a short guy in uniform, with three stars on his shoulder. It seemed a long time before I knew it was the *político* from Acapulco. I got it, then, that order to lay off the gringo. He couldn't shoot me. I was too important. But he could shoot her, for trying to escape, or resisting arrest, or whatever it was. And he could stand there, and wait, and get his kick when I had to look at her.

I jumped for him, and he stepped back, but then I turned to water, and I sank down beside her, the cops, the lights, and the ambulance going around and around in a horrible spin. If he had done that to her, what had I done?

Once more I was in the vestry room of the little church near Acapulco, and I could even see the burned place on the bricks where we had made the fire. Indians were slipping in barefooted, the women with *rebozos* over their heads, the men in white suits, extra clean. Her father and mother were in the first pew, and some sisters and brothers I didn't even know she had. The casket was white, and the altar was banked with the flowers I had had sent down, flowers from Xochimilco, that she liked. The choir loft was full of boys and girls, all in white. The priest came in, started to put on his vestments, and I paid him. He caught my arm. "You sing, yes, Señor Sharp? An *Agnus Dei* perhaps?"

"No."

He shrugged, turned away, and pulled the surplice over his head. This horrible sense of guilt swept over me, like it had a hundred times in the last two days. ". . . Never. . . . Never again."

"Ah."

He just breathed it, and stood looking at me, then his hand traced a blessing for me, and he whispered in Latin. I knew, then, I had made a confession, and received an absolution, and some kind of gray peace came over me. I went out, slipped in the pew with her family, and the music started. They carried her out to a grave on the hillside. As they lowered her down, an iguana jumped out of it and went running over the rocks.

JAMES M. CAIN (1892-1977) is recognized today as one of the masters of the hard-boiled school of American novels. Born in Baltimore, the son of the president of Washington College, he began his career as reporter on the Baltimore papers, served in the American Expeditionary Force in World War I and wrote the material for *The Cross of Lorraine*, the newspaper of the 79th Division. He returned to become professor of journalism at St. John's College in Annapolis and then worked for H.L. Mencken on *The American Mercury*. He later wrote editorials for Walter Lippman on the *New York World* and was for a short period managing editor of *The New Yorker*, before he went to Hollywood as a script writer. His first novel, *The Postman Always Rings Twice*, was published when he was forty-two and at once became a sensation. It was tried for obscenity in Boston, was said by Albert Camus to have inspired his own book, *The Stranger*, and is now a classic. Cain followed it the next year with *Double Indemnity*, leading Ross MacDonald to write years later, "Cain has won unfading laurels with a pair of native American masterpieces, *Postman* and *Double Indemnity*, back to back." Cain published eighteen books in all and was working on his autobiography at the time of his death.